Tit for Tat

AUDREY HOPKINS

Scripture Union

Other books by this author
Love and Laura – *Impressions* series
One for Sorrow – *Impressions* series
Over the Edge – *Impressions* series
September Secret – *Leopard* series
The Worst of Friends – *Leopard* series
Double Trouble – *6–8s*

© Audrey Hopkins 1996
First published 1996

Published by Scripture Union, 207–209 Queensway, Bletchley,
Milton Keynes, MK2 2EB, England.

ISBN 1 85999 001 0

British Library Cataloguing-in-Publication Data.
A catalogue record for this book is available from the British Library.

Phototypeset by Intype London Ltd.
Printed and bound in Great Britain by Cox & Wyman Ltd, Reading.

Contents

~ 1 ~

Chris . . . on Nick

'Am I my brother's keeper?' Not on your life I'm not! I might be older than he is but that doesn't mean I'm responsible for him, does it? If he insists on acting the complete and utter idiot I'm not going to stop him. Why should I?

He's up there on the terrapin roof!

Funny thing, that – calling a flat-roofed, oblong porta-classroom a terrapin. It looks nothing like 'any of various web-footed reptiles that live on land and in fresh water and feed on small aquatic animals,' or so the dictionary says.

Anyway, as I said, he's up there on the terrapin roof, sunbathing, and everybody's eyeing me as if it's *my* fault! I didn't put the twit up to it and, believe me, if I *had* he'd never have done it, just to be as awkward as possible.

That's how we are, Nick and me, always doing the opposite and usually at each other's throats. I can't stand him and he detests me – don't ask me why. I'm an easy-going sort of guy and I don't start it, honest!

He's just a pig-headed big-head, that's all.

I'm Chris Barrat and I'm fifteen, just. Nick is my brother – well, he isn't, technically. We do have the same mother and father, his by birth and mine by adoption, so we belong to the same family – not that you'd notice! We're so different we could have been born on different planets!

Legally, if not physically, we're brothers and I'm the elder by a year and a bit. Nick is fourteen going on four and acts it, though he *is* taller than me – and takes advantage of it. How I've suffered at his hands because of those extra inches! The nerd!

I suppose it's all in the genes, the DNA stuff. Nick looks a lot like Dad – big hands, long legs and a way of moving as if he has twice as many joints as normal people . . . sort of shambling and loose. He always looks as if everything's just too much trouble to be bothered with and sails through life doing nothing. The only time he perks up is when he spots – what he calls – a tasty chick, and they're usually blonde. He goes for blondes and the dimmer the better. 'Give me a bimbo any day,' he says. Personally, I prefer a girl to have something upstairs, a brain and a personality you can communicate with. I tell him . . . 'Girls aren't just to look at, they're people with ideas and convictions!'

'Bull!' he says.

They say 'all the world's a stage' and they're not far wrong where Nick's concerned. He's always acting the tough guy, the hard man who cares for nothing and nobody unless there's something in it for him. Maybe he isn't acting? He shambles about as if he hasn't a care in the world. His hair flops over his eyes and he flips it back with an arrogant toss of his big head, putting the teachers' backs up and usually dropping *me* in it.

'Christopher,' they say, in their condescending voices, 'Nicholas can be very disruptive in class. Can you have a word with him?'

I always feel like asking: which word would you suggest? Aardvark . . . Anchovy . . . Wally? But I don't. They wouldn't see the comedy, would they?

The only words I'd like to say to Nicholas are, 'Get off my back, brother! I'm sick of your stupid stunts and I'm fed up with carrying the can for them.' Trouble is, he's too tall to tangle with!

Me . . . I'm short − sort of. Not short beside the others in my class, you understand − just short compared with Nick and that's no joke.

People always think he's the oldest and that's even less of a rib-tickler!

Usually, when they've been put right on that score, it's, 'You don't look a bit like brothers (snicker-snicker). You're so − well − dark.'

You can hear the implied question.

I suppose I could go into an explanation of my ethnic mix but why should I? They don't. We've got kids with names like sneezes but nobody asks them which East European enclave they've escaped from! Half of me's Indian actually. My other half is Scottish, so I understand. I have black hair and very dark brown eyes but the rest of me isn't all that out of the ordinary − except that I get a great tan in the summer and it lasts till spring! That causes a bit of aggro, me bronzed and handsome all winter!

Let's face it, we don't look alike and there's no reason why we should. We don't think alike or feel alike either, and neither of us has any desire to change things, believe me.

We beg to differ, always have.

When we were kids we were always in trouble but, most of the time, it was me that took the rap. Not because it was *me*, you understand, but because I was the one who ended up shoeless, coatless, wet through, muddied, torn and often bleeding. He egged me on, that's what he did . . . got me doing things I didn't want to do but had to because he said I couldn't. He always bet I couldn't leap something or climb something as well as he could and I couldn't let that go, could I? Most times he never did the things anyway, because I went first – to prove myself – usually came a cropper and he couldn't do anything for laughing!

It was all Nick's fault. He came out of every scrape unscathed, smiling like an overweight Botticelli cherub, with his fair hair and blue eyes. Mummy's little angel!

Whatever he did, or *said* he could do, I had to go one better and usually took on far more than I could handle. Over the years I've been in the canal fully clothed, in the river fully clothed and halfway up the derelict Bethel Chapel wall and scared stiff of falling – and all because Nick said he could swing over the canal on a rope and scale the chapel wall as easily as falling off a log – which, incidentally, is why I was in the river. My log rolled!

I suppose, if I'm totally honest, I'm jealous. He's bigger, stronger and – let's face it – there must be something in this 'flesh of my flesh' thing – you know, the 'blood's thicker than water' idea that's supposed to unite families – because he seems to get away with everything, at home as well as at school where the teachers shake their heads, 'tut tut' a bit then let him off. I don't know what it is he's got!

Nick says it's his good looks, natural charm and winning ways. I say they've given up on him, they can't be bothered because he's not worth losing sleep over, that he's a loser . . . and then the tiff becomes a tussle and I run for it. That's one thing I *am* better at – running. I've had to be! Faced with half a dozen yobs bent on a 'blackie-bash' it's the only thing to do . . . run like the wind. There's no use protesting, it doesn't make any difference.

I'm better than Nick at school work too, considerably. I get straight As for most subjects. My only B subject is English and that's only because I have a slight problem with spelling . . . nothing serious. I'm brilliant, orally. I suppose I'm more of a maths and science type, with a bit of geography thrown in.

Geography's useful to a pilot.

Nick's lucky if he gets a mark at all! Most times he doesn't hand work in and when he does it's a pathetic attempt. He's just not bothered. 'I'll get by,' he says, with a wink and that infuriating hair-flick. He usually does!

Take this morning.

We get up at the usual time and I'm first in the bathroom – because he refuses to get out of bed until the last possible minute – but I've hardly started before he's hammering on the door. It's locked, otherwise he'd barge in and throw me out, so all he can do is hammer and holler.

'Out, flea-bite!' he says, with menace.

'Get lost, turnip-head,' I mumble, mouth frothy with toothpaste – and there's a funny story . . .

Our dippy mum goes to every chemist in town asking for that new toothpaste that's advertised on TV.

'A tube of *Wow* please,' she says. 'Family size.'

Nobody's heard of this *Wow* stuff but she insists it's advertised on the telly and tells them they're not keeping up with new trends, until the girl in Boots tells her it isn't called 'Wow'; that it's just the people on the advert expressing their delight because it's good stuff and she produces a tube called something entirely different.

WOW! Did we laugh – me *and* Nick!

Anyway – there's me with a mouth full of toothpaste and he's hammering on the door.

'Out now, or your maths project's in the shredder,' he says.

'What shredder?' I mutter, spitting into the sink.

'This shredder,' he says and I hear paper tearing and he's munching away making lip-smacking yummy sounds. He's eating my maths project!

Naturally, with a term's work going down his epiglottis, I charge out of the bathroom and leap on him, just as Mum (wouldn't you know it?) turns the corner at the top of the stairs and I get screamed at while he stands, grinning, and not a shred of paper in sight!

'He's eating my maths project,' I protest, glaring at him and foaming at the mouth.

'He's mad, Mum. Rabid!' Nick says, shrugging his shoulders and lifting his hands in innocent denial. 'Chill out, Chris. I haven't even *seen* your maths project.' And he goes into the bathroom and locks the door.

'When are you going to grow up?' Mum says. 'Your homework's on the sideboard where you left it. If you tidied away after yourself you'd know where things are. Your bedroom's a tip!'

'*My* bedroom's a tip? Have you seen his?' I protest, aggrieved.

'I'm talking about you, not Nick,' she says, and that just about says it all – me in the wrong and frothing at the mouth while he sings in the bathroom just to annoy me a bit more. Actually, *sing* is the wrong word. Nick *raps*! He knows I hate it and Reggae and Soul!

We argue all the way to school. It's a good ten minutes

walk to the bus followed by half an hour of stopping and starting through town and out to The Broadway. That's where Cannongate High is now. It got too big for the old Gothic building in town. The new building does have its good points . . . like an all-weather sports field and track and the biggest sports hall in the county.

We only just catch the bus, because he dawdles just to make me mad, and I tell him he gets away with murder.

'Not yet,' he says, and grins.

I don't think I've ever seen him without that stupid smirk *he* thinks is so attractive.

After assembly we always have ten minutes to spare before first lesson. It's supposed to be a social time where we can 'interact' and read any new notices on the boards. The Junior area is just a concrete playground surrounded by Block A, the Sports Hall and the Science Block with the tennis courts on the fourth side and very chilly in winter. The Senior Quad is in the centre of the main school, totally enclosed by classrooms and concrete. It's a bit like a cloister with a covered walk all round and paving in the middle bit that's open to the sky – but don't get the idea that it's all arches and rustic stone pillars. Girders and glass is a better description! The old school did have arches and stained glass in the Quad so I suppose it's reasonable to have kept the name and the tradition.

All the activity boards are on the west wall – sports, music, art and various other lunch-time clubs while the 'Today' board is on the south side, next to the opening that leads to the Head's study and the offices.

It's always full, the Quad, because it's better than queuing up outside classrooms when the corridors are full of people trying to get to their lockers. What idiot thought of lining the school's arteries with lockers, I ask you?

So, the Quad is a favourite place to hang about in, except in the middle. That's where the 'pairs' stand, when it's not raining. It's like a public announcement: 'We're an item, back off!'

I've never been in the middle.

This morning, we're in the Quad, hugging the wall as usual and I'm talking to Gaz . . . Gary Cooper. His nan wanted him called Gary after some old movie star she had a crush on and he detests it. Can't say I blame him. I'm telling Gaz that I haven't finished a piece of course-work and it's due in third lesson. Gaz is just suggesting some good excuses – the cat was sick on it, Ma spilt soup over it, etc – when Nick comes up behind us.

'Bunk off!' he says.

Gaz and me stare at him, like he's something out of the funny farm.

'Miss third lesson,' he goes on. 'Want some good places?'

'You talk rubbish, Nick. Ignore him, Gaz.'

I should have kept my mouth clamped!

'Chicken!' Nick taunts, trying to sneer and grin at the same time and the result resembles the end gargoyle on St Kentigern's porch – ugly and twisted! 'I've done it loads!'

'You're all talk, Barrat,' Gaz says and I try to back off through the wall before Nick throws a punch. He's done it for less.

He doesn't! He grins, moves off and the next time I spot him he's on the terrapin roof! His class is listening to History Humphreys and trying not to laugh while he's hanging upside down outside the window and baring his fangs like a vampire bat. More like a fruit bat, if you ask me . . . totally bananas!

He's still up there when Miss Humphreys stops me and asks if my brother's ill. I can see him, still grinning and she's waiting for an answer so I tell her I don't know and try to keep a straight face. It isn't easy!

'You don't know?' she says, in that condescending 'I'm constantly amazed at the idiocy of the young' voice that teachers have. It must be part of their training. I can just picture them, standing in rows, striking a pose and saying it, in unison.

'You don't know?' she repeats. 'You came to school on your own this morning? Don't you communicate with the other members of your family?'

I could kill him. There's nothing I can say without looking a right nerd and she's telling me off for dumb insolence while he's having hysterics on the roof.

'I left before him,' I mumble, when she lets me get a word in, and she goes off to investigate.

They have a sixth sense, teachers – a built-in warning system that tells them you're lying.

'Good on yer, Bro,' Nick says, loping across to me after dropping off the terrapin and bowing to his junior fan club, who cheer. What an example to the young!

'Beat that!' he says, thumping my shoulder.

'You're in for it if she rings home,' I tell him, but he shrugs.

'I'll think of something,' he says – winking, walking off and licking his finger to give himself a stripe on his blazer sleeve.

One up on me, is he?

I can't ignore it. It's like a knight throwing down his lady's glove in challenge; you have to take up the gauntlet – don't you?

15

Third lesson, and Mr Ingram says I can have another week to finish the course-work because I'm well ahead and my marks are consistently good. Then, at break, Dickie Dixon – general studies – says I can miss the afternoon triple and go for an interview. I've a week's work experience coming up and I've asked for the path' lab at the General Hospital. It's a career I might consider if I don't make pilot or oceanographer.

I'd forgotten Dad had signed a consent form at the beginning of term, a 'Parental Permission to be off the premises' sort of thing. It was a chance to get one up on Brother Dork!

'I'm bunking off for the afternoon,' I tell him at lunch-time – looking nonchalant.

'No way, brother. You haven't the guts,' he sneers.

'Watch me,' I say and saunter out through the main gates while he stands, gobsmacked, in the dinner queue.

Howzat, brother?

I have a topping afternoon chatting to a junior pathologist who asks why I fancy the work and shows me round. It's a bit stomach churning, looking at bits in bottles, but no more so than flying a jet at Mach 2 and a mile high or filming Great Whites in the ocean. Mostly, it's checking blood and tissue samples on glass slides and I have a look through a microscope.

Amazing!

When I get home, Nick isn't grinning. His eyes have gone steely grey and his fists are clenched, a very bad sign – for me.

'Upstairs!' he says and, as I have to change out of school clothes, I go – not because he said I should. Mum's in and she hates it when we argue. She looks all pained and disappointed when we scrap so we try to keep our battles as private as possible. I suspect she knows we have our differences but plays them down in her own mind.

'What's your problem?' I say, slinging my bag on my bed and trying not to look him in the eye – that can be dangerous.

'You pulled a fast one,' he says, scowling at me from the doorway.

We have a pact, one of many, that says bedrooms are out of bounds to brothers. So far he hasn't broken it but today might just be the day. He's mad!

'So?' I say. 'What's the problem?'

'You're the problem,' he says. 'You cheated!'

'Chill out, Nick,' I say, glaring at his feet (not his eyes). 'Go and play with your motor cars.'

He collects *Corgi* and *Matchbox* miniatures and hates being accused of playing with them.

'I said, you cheated,' he goes on, putting one toe over the demarcation line.

'Cross that line and you'll get it,' I threaten.

'Come over here and say that,' he says, and he puts a whole foot in my room!

Now, here *is* a dilemma. If I don't go out, he'll come in and sanctuary will be lost for ever. If I go out, he'll batter me!

One time, during a ruck, he held me over the banister rail by the ankles. I was really small, then. I've grown quite a bit, this last year, but I'm still no match for Nick. Not when he's mad.

Still, sanctuary must be maintained, whatever the cost.

I put my head down and charge.

'Get your big foot out of my room,' I grunt as my head connects with his solar plexus.

'Woomph!' he gasps, staggering backwards and winded. Then, before he gets his breath back and can

17

retaliate, Mum's on the landing with an armful of clean washing.

'What's going on?' she asks.

'Not a lot,' Nick says, clutching his stomach. 'Must be the hamburger I had for lunch.'

'Junk food!' Mum says, eyeing us both as if she's not convinced and waiting for something to happen. We can't just walk away, can we?

'Here, Chris,' Nick says, pulling a note out of his pocket. 'Mr Dixon asked me to deliver it. It's about what they did this afternoon, while you were at the hospital.' Then he goes in his room and shuts the door.

So, that's how he knows I didn't bunk off!

'Hospital?' Mum shrieks, eyebrows shooting to the top of her head.

'Work experience, Mum,' I explain and she thrusts half the washing at me.

'I never know with you two,' she says. 'Put those away and get changed. Tea won't be long.'

Then she goes and taps on Nick's door and tells him she's got his clean shirts and will he *please* come out and take them. Notice the difference?

I get changed into jeans and T-shirt and find one of his in my pile – but he can whistle for it!

At tea we talk about the day and my visit to the hospital. I don't mention Nick's roof-sit and he doesn't say I head-butted him. It's an unwritten code, you see. Mum and Dad think all's well with the world and us – and that's how we keep it, when possible. Most brothers have their differences, I would think, and most parents understand that – surely?

'Am I my brother's keeper?' Not likely, but we do try to keep the *family* peace. It's the one thing we agree on – the one joint effort in our disjointed relationship.

~ 2 ~

Nick . . . on Chris

Anybody who listens to my brother Chris is as much a
nerd as he is! He spins lies like spiders spin webs.

It's the same old story – every morning. Chris gets to
the bathroom first and I'm hanging about on the landing.

He must set his alarm for half past five, just to get one
up on me. It's his main aim in life, getting one up on
me – and mine to see that he doesn't!

I'm a night person. I don't get tired at parties and do
my best and most original work after midnight.

They – that mysterious 'they' that are always being
quoted – say it all depends on the hour of your birth. I'm
an after midnight person, born at two in the morning. I
like staying up late and hate getting up in the morning.
I suppose I ought to consider night work as a profession.

Chris is just the opposite, as he is in most things. I
bet he was born at six in the morning, because that's
when he's up and about and making unnecessary noises
just to annoy me.

I wouldn't mind him getting to the bathroom first,

but he dawdles – messes about – just to be awkward. It's not as if he's got a girlfriend to impress. He's always got his big nose in a book and, to my knowledge, books aren't one bit impressed by clean teeth and aftershave.

Aftershave! He puts it on every morning and his chin's never seen a razor! He does my head in!

Actually, I can't think what I've done to upset him. We were mates, once, me and our Chris. We used to have great times. Some of them were a bit hairy but I didn't come to any harm. He's a year and five months older than me and I was a bit of a porker as a kid. I didn't walk until I was two, so Mum tells me, and I never said much. I used to sit around and let him use me as a guinea-pig: mustard sandwiches, biro tattoos, food colouring for the hair and other examples of good clean fun, or so he said. Once, he wired me to a sequence of batteries and was just about to push the other end of the wire into a power point when Mum found us. I don't remember making a comment but I'm told I said, 'Chrissy's making a bomb!'

It was my first complete sentence – subject-verb-predicate – and it's one of those stories that comes up every Christmas, when Gran and Gramps are around and to my everlasting embarrassment!

We used to do things together, me and Chris, until he got this huge chip on his shoulder and blamed me – nice guy Nick – for his own problems.

I've got problems of my own, like most handsome 'hero' types. I have to fight off the girls and stop the juniors from kneeling at my feet in total adoration, don't I?

'Let's do this,' Chris used to say. 'Let's do that.' And I went along and did it, because that's the amiable sort of chap I am. It's easier to go with the flow than swim against the tide, isn't it? The fact that he couldn't hack it, couldn't put his money where his mouth was, was nothing to do with me – I didn't sling him in the canal!

He's got big ideas, my brother Chris, and has a nasty habit of biting off more than he can chew. He's always trying to *prove* himself, prove he's better than me. He *is* better, in some things, but I don't get my knickers in a twist because of it. Who cares?

By the time I was old enough to realise I *had* a brother, he could walk, run and catch a ball better than anybody else around – when all I could do was sit on the floor and drool. I wasn't jealous . . . I like sitting and I liked watching him. I was actually proud of the nerd, would you believe it?

When I was five and he was six, our dad got us membership of a swimming club. Harrison's Herons, we were called, though why herons I can't imagine. They don't swim, do they? Anyway – we joined this club and it wasn't more than a week before Chris was streaking up the pool like a baby barracuda. It wasn't exactly crawl but it was near it. Old Harrison was gobsmacked.

'Look at him go!' he yelled, and I felt great. There was my brother, beating bigger fish than he was while I was floundering in the shallows and trying to get up enough courage to be a starfish and take my feet off the deck! I was proud, would you believe it? Nobody shouted louder than me when he took trophy after trophy.

What happened, you ask?

I'll tell you what happened – we went to school and people noticed we weren't exactly similar. I suppose I put my foot in it when I told the class he was an eastern-type prince. He was, to me, but they didn't believe me and started picking on him.

My brother Chris picks fights when there's nothing to fight about – nothing important, anyway. To be honest, I don't care about the bathroom thing, not really. It's Chris that makes an issue out of it.

I have a philosophy, which is a big word for Nick Barrat – who's supposed to be thick. I believe in playing it cool and for laughs – and why not?

Oh, I know all about 'getting qualifications' and all that jazz, but I don't know what I want . . . yet. I don't want to be pigeon-holed, filed under 'white-collar professional' or 'mucky-handed mechanic'. When I know, for sure, what I want, then I'll go for it with all guns blazing. Until then, I'll keep my options open, thank you. Life's supposed to be a ball, isn't it?

Look at Chris! He's charging about doing so many different things that he doesn't know whether he's coming or going, half the time. He goes to ATC because he wants to fly, scuba-dives on Wednesdays in case Jacques Cousteau or someone similar should desire his presence in a shark cage on a sea quest, and runs three miles, most nights, because an Olympic gold is not out of the question and it wouldn't half make Mum proud.

Then, as if all that isn't enough, he chooses to visit a path lab in case he decides to go into medicine! That would please Dad, who'd be as proud as Mum, if he had a son who's a doctor. What's Chris trying to prove? That he's an all-round genius? He really does my head in, and it isn't because I can't think of anything that might make them proud of me! And – I ask you – does it matter?

Get a life, Bro – that's *my* advice, for what it's worth. There's things to do and even more things to think about – 'More things in heaven and earth, Horatio, than are dreamt of in your philosophy'. (And that proves I'm not a dork!)

I do have a long-term plan, but I'm not pushing it — yet. I might change my mind. Everybody changes. I wanted to be a racing driver when I was six and a chef when I was nine!

Old Chris has so many strings to his bow, he'll end up with every arrow missing its mark — and I'm supposed to be the dork, the loser!

Besides, he's his own worst enemy.

Take this morning, just as one example among many. I get him out of the bathroom, eventually, and we get ready for school. I can't find my clean shirt and he has it, so there's a bit of a ruck before we go downstairs . . . nothing serious, mind you, just a bit of jostling and a few dirty looks that we turn into smiles as we hit the kitchen. We don't speak on the bus, which isn't unusual, and when we get to the school gate there's an evil-looking crowd blocking it.

Now I, sensing the mob's mood with extrasensory perception (the clenched fists and twisted grins, actually), sidestep the nearest dork and vault the low wall. I land in the bushes but it's no sweat. A quick shoe-wipe on the grass and I'm ready for anything the day can throw at me.

But not Christopher Barrat, not he! Big brother has to play the big guy, the Senior Form Prefect, no less, and a figure of authority. It says so on his badge. Ha!

I try to get his attention but he's intent on having his way and starting World War Three!

'Step aside,' he says to the nearest yobbo. Unfortunately, for Chris, the nearest yobbo just happens to be Keith Beasley, who's been excluded twice for fighting. Exclusion means three days cooling your heels at home till your mum and dad promise you'll behave, and then it's interviews with the Head and 'contracts' to sign —

lists of agreed rules, etc. Apart from the hassle, it isn't brave to face up to Beasley, it's suicidal!

'Who's asking?' Beasley says, squaring up.

'I'm not asking. I'm telling,' Chris says, and I get behind the gatepost. Is he completely bonkers?

'Rack off, Sambo!' Beasley says, spitting a mouthful of pink gum on to the pavement.

Now that puts my back up. It's nothing to do with being brothers – Chris asks for trouble much of the time – it's to do with the race thing. So what if he's half Indian or something? It's nobody's business but his . . . ours! Making racial remarks is just not on! It's school policy, actually. Being on the edge of the city, Cannongate has quite an ethnic mix and it's drilled into us from Year One that prejudice, of any kind, is a definite 'no-no'. Besides, we've got a Headmaster who's as dark as Chris!

The rest of Beasley's gang square up behind him and I'm just about to wade in and scatter a few – just like I would for anybody being picked on and in the minority – when Chris legs it, up the road to the side entrance, followed by jeers and more name-calling.

And that's Chris all over. He starts something but doesn't hang around to finish it.

I hate to say it, but he asks for all he gets. All he had to do was vault the wall and avoid the whole hoo-hah. Isn't prevention better than cure?

We had a sermon in church last Sunday. The Rev told us that we should love our enemies and not retaliate if we're attacked. It makes us as bad as the attacker! I know what he means . . . we shouldn't hit back but turn the other cheek to show that fighting proves and solves nothing – which is really hard to do if somebody is smashing your face in.

Chris shouldn't have got himself in that situation, but as he *had*, he'd have done better if he'd stood his ground, got in first and knocked the smirk off Beasley's face then taken a pasting like a man. He'd have been thought better of.

As it is, he's legging it up the field with half of Year Nine after him, whooping it up like Geronimo's tribe on a scalping spree. (I'm into native North American culture and history!)

We meet up in the Senior Quad and he has a go at me.

'Where were you?' he says. 'You're supposed to be the school "hit man", the big hero, the protector of the underdog!'

'Not my business,' I tell him. 'Besides, you asked for it. You always have to act top dog and you can't back it up!'

'Oh yeah!' he says, tossing his arrogant head and strutting. 'You're *all* talk, Nick old boy. You've got nothing going for you. Nothing! You're a loser.'

Now that does make me mad and I grab him by his prefect's tie and yank him up to *my* height.

'You're the loser,' I tell him. 'But you're so pig-headed you just don't see it, or won't!'

I put him down, then – because he's going purple – and he straightens his tie. Always the neat dude is our Chris.

'Any brother worth his salt would've waded in and demolished them,' he says.

'On my own?' I say, grinning. 'You were long gone, old son, and it wasn't *my* battle!'

'I'd have gone in . . . with a bit of backing,' Chris says, combing his hair.

'Bodyguards cost money,' I tell him, walking away

because everybody's moving off to lessons. 'And I come expensive!'

I know it isn't the thing to do, the Christian thing, but I can't help it. There's something about the little dork that brings out the beast in me.

Things seem to get worse the older we are. We used to have fun, sort of. It used to be merry rivalry – each of us trying to score points and getting a kick out of being top dog, even slapping each other on the back. We haven't done that this term. It's all become so serious.

So far, I've bunked off a lesson and got away with it. One-nil to me. I'm not allowing Chris's afternoon among the specimen bottles. That was cheating.

Last term, we had a good laugh. I'd done a couple of stunts that caused a bit of a flutter in the staff-room, like printing an 'official' letter from the governors and posting it on the teachers' board in the Quad. They thought they were really having a full inspection – for about ten minutes! Laugh? They were dashing about like ants under aardvark attack, (I have a liking for aardvarks) and almost exploded when they discovered it was a sneaky ruse.

But, and I have to admit it, Chris got the invisible Oscar for his tuck shop scam. He put a notice on the 'Today' board, advertising succulent goodies for sale – in the maths room at break.

There's nobody as staid and meticulously tidy as our maths teacher. Perfect Price we call him.

There wasn't a tuck shop, naturally, but at break the corridor outside the maths suite was packed, all the way to the fire doors and Perfect Pricey couldn't get out for his mid-morning trip to the staff-room. He goes totally ape without his caffeine fix.

He was barking mad! There were juniors everywhere,

climbing over each other to be one of the first ten customers who – Chris had promised – were getting a free flapjack. It was chaos! Price was screaming, the kids were yelling and we nearly passed out, laughing!

One up to Chris, that was.

At break, I run into Carrie Anders in the canteen.

Not *actually* running into her, you understand. More of a 'coming up behind her in the queue' sort of thing. There's no sign of Chris and I suspect he's button-holed some over-worked teacher and is plying him with intelligent questions that the poor man can't answer. It's one of the things Chris enjoys. It's his hobby. Would you believe that he spends hours devouring books of 'interesting and obscure facts' just to put one over on the teachers? Personally, I don't communicate with them at all, if I can help it. They're only people, aren't they? They can't be expected to know everything . . . like Chris thinks he does, the geek!

When we get to a table, Carrie rabbits on about some film that's showing at the Odeon and how she's got no one to go with, and – while I'm trying to get away because I can't afford to take her and she might not think of paying for herself – I get this fabulous idea.

'So, what do you think?' Carrie is saying, and I'm not sure what the question is! She's not bad, as girls go, but she's got brown hair, and gentlemen, like me, prefer blondes and I have to live up to my legend!

'About what?' I say, all wide-eyed and innocent.

'About going to see this film with me?'

She looks all soft and lovely and I almost give in, but it would mean extricating the loot from dear brother Chris and I'd have to hit him. Now if Carrie had been a blonde . . .!

'No dosh,' I say, looking suitably apologetic and turning out both trouser pockets.

'I'm pretty flush – enough for two, anyway,' Carrie says, blushing. 'No strings, or anything like that. I just don't fancy going by myself. The Odeon's always packed with unattached nerds.'

I know what she's on about. The place is always thick with last year's leavers, the unemployed masses. One thing's for sure . . . I might not know where I'm going – as yet – but I'm definitely going somewhere, and not into a dole queue! Anyway, back to Carrie . . .

'Never!' I say, shaking my handsome head. 'Sponging off *ein gnädiges Fräulein ist verboten*! (I'm not too bad at German, but for the uni-lingual, it means: 'letting a lovely girlie pay for me is not cricket!') Why don't you ask Chris?'

I saunter away and I'm sorry she looks hurt and abandoned, but I'm not into this bodyguard thing for her or Chris. It's a difficult life, being an Adonis!

Besides, I've got this fabulous idea and it won't wait. I filch some sheets of paper from the teachers' photocopying room on the bottom corridor and write a notice . . . best script, of course. It has to look authentic.

ARE YOU UNATTACHED?
At a loose end and generally untied?
SAY NO MORE!
Anyone interested in creating a data bank
for the purpose of forming a Computer Dating Agency,
should meet in the Lower Hall at 1pm.
Interests considered.
BE THERE!

I have to get it on to the 'Today' board without being seen, but that's no problem for Nicky-boy Barrat.

By this time, I'm in Peter Potter's English class, having spent the first ten minutes writing the thing and totally missing his introduction to *Withering Heights*, or is it *Wuthering*? . . . and does anybody care?

'Sir,' I say, pulling a face and clutching my jaw. I'm very convincing when I want to be – destined for stardom, perhaps?

Potter peers over his rimless half-specs.

'What seems to be the problem, Barrat?' he asks, plodding down the aisle in his old, checked slippers. He always wears them in school, some say to creep up on us while we're working – just to make sure that we are – but I think he's got corns and bunions. He walks like he's treading on hot coals.

'Tooth, sir,' I grunt, rubbing my jaw and pulling an agonised face. 'Can I go for a painkiller?'

'*May* I go, if you please, Barrat. *May I*!' he says, eyes raised to the ceiling and fingers pressed together like a praying mantis. ' "Can I" means "am I able to" and as you have legs, feet and the required musculature to manipulate them efficiently, I assume you *can* go for the painkiller! The question is, shall I *allow* you to go?'

'Will you, sir?'

'And that's another little quirk in the English language, Barrat – shall I . . . will I? "Shall I" suggests a personal dilemma while . . .'

'It really hurts, sir!' I groan, in desperation and amid the semi-stifled giggles of English Set C.

' "Pearls before swine", Barrat. "Pearls before swine",' he says, shaking his head. 'Go, if you must.'

'Thanks, sir,' I say, smiling because he's a nice enough old wrinkly, as wrinklies go.

There's no one about in the Quad, it being lesson time, so I stick the notice up and head to the admin office for the pill – just in case Potter checks up, which is doubtful. He doesn't remember where *he* is, half the time, let alone where *we* are? I don't suppose he'd notice if I was gone the whole lesson but I'm back in less than five minutes and there's just an hour to go before the fun begins.

Hilarious!

By five past one the Lower Hall's packed to capacity. The corridor's jammed and a horde of screaming juniors, the whole lower school by the look of it, are pressed against the outer windows – squashed noses ignored – trying to see what's going on.

There's hardly anyone in the canteen. Two minuscule new kids, girls, I think – I can't see their legs and it's hard to tell from their jerseys and short hair – are at the serving hatch and a very spotty senior, with buck teeth, is solemnly kicking the drinks machine.

He has a great sense of rhythm!

Francesca Wells, who is so upper crust she wouldn't touch any of us with a ten foot pole, is eating her packed lunch at a table by the window.

I don't fancy my chances . . . I don't even fancy her, but I give it a try, anyway. Somebody has to have a crack at melting the ice-maiden.

'Not joining the dating agency?' I ask her, strolling up with a can and a sandwich and giving her my most winning smile. It usually has them on their knees!

Not this time!

She gives me such a look – one that's supposed to make a guy shrivel up and disappear in a puff of smoke – but I'm made of sterner stuff and sit down at her table and flash my pearly teeth. That usually gets them.

She doesn't say a word, just looks down her nose and leaves.

30

If there *was* such a thing as a dating agency, I'd rig the computer to fix her up with Chris. They'd suit each other!

Lunch-time is absolute chaos. Half the staff are *outside* the hall, trying to clear the corridor. The other half are *inside*, trying to get the senior school *outside*; while the juniors, who are *outside*, are trying to get *inside* to find out what's happening. The din is terrific, inside and out!

I leave them to it, not failing to notice that Chris is in there, helping the teachers – typical!

Carrie's in the Quad.

'You didn't go to the meeting, then?' I ask.

'Not likely,' she says. 'It's pathetic, dating by numbers. It's humiliating.'

And to think I did it for her. Women!

She watches me write on the white-board.

NB Two – Nil.

A good ruse, is that. To the uninitiated, NB is just 'note well' or *nota bene* in Latin. The fact that they're my initials will only be noticed by Chris!

'What's that mean?' Carrie asks, and I notice that, when she's puzzled, her nose crinkles and her lips pucker up. Cute or what?

I just grin and tap my nose, not to tell her to keep *her* nose out, you understand. Just to say it's a bit of a secret.

Chris will know exactly what it means. We've been counting our victories since we were kids.

At one time we had a blackboard and we chalked them up on that. Later, when we'd done with chalks and crayons, we fastened bottle-tops on our jerseys and wore the badges with pride. Mum wasn't too keen on that period though — too many holey jerseys!

Nowadays we use invisible stripes on our sleeves. Chris has a real one on his ATC uniform, but that's a different ball game.

One time — and it was only once — Chris had an armful of victories. That was because he was older. There's a much wider gap between two and going on four than there is between fourteen and fifteen plus. It's wider when you're smaller. At four, Chris could catch a ball, hit it with a bat and kick a football in a net. And he could run. He would jump ropes, too, when I was too fat and just about capable of a slow waddle.

Since then, I've been ahead on points, not counting the academic side and he can have that — it's not my scene.

School is late starting, not surprisingly, and I come face to face with Chris in the upper corridor.

'Prat!' he says.

'What makes you so sure it was me?' I ask, grinning.

'Who else? I've missed a quarter of Jenkin's tutorial and it was important!'

'Get your priorities right, brother,' I retort, and duck as he throws a punch.

'Missed!' I taunt, and head for drama. I don't suppose it's the end of the affair but — I've proved a point. I've got what it takes and he hasn't.

Over to you . . . brother!

~ *3* ~

Loggerheads

The rivalry between the Barrat brothers didn't go unnoticed – not at school, anyway. They were often the topic of conversation among the various groups and cliques that frequented the staff-room. Usually, as a result of an occurrence involving the two boys, even the closest of cliques was divided. There were those who liked Chris and those who favoured Nick.

'I've a feeling that yesterday's chaos had something to do with Christopher Barrat,' Mr Price said, looking down his nose. 'Another episode like his tuck shop joke, last term. I've never forgiven him for that débâcle.'

'Doubt it, it sounds more like Nick to me – a dating agency! Just like him!' Mrs Bailey said, shaking her head and smiling.

Mrs Bailey taught drama and theatre studies and had a *very* soft spot for Nick, who seemed able to take on any role from Romeo to Sweeney Todd, the demon barber.

'Well, it went up in the Senior Quad, some time

between morning break and lunch-time. Someone had to be out of lessons to do it,' Mr Grange pointed out. 'And nobody left *my* room, that's for sure. If I can't leave my class unattended to visit the toilet, why should they?'

'I had Chris Barrat over break and all three lessons after! We had a complicated experiment to set up and see through,' Mr Otley chipped in.

'So – who *was* out of lessons?' Mr Price asked the question everybody was thinking. 'Who had *Nick* Barrat?'

A quick look at the timetable board, bristling with coloured pins and flags, sent Mr Price to Mr Potter, where he sat marking books.

'Nick Barrat?' Mr Potter said, confused at first. 'Yesterday, when . . . after break? Ah! Had a bad tooth-ache – real pain – you could see it in his face. Went for an aspirin, period five.'

'Ha!' Mr Price said, nodding triumphantly. 'I knew it had to be one or the other of the Barrat boys. It's a shame . . . their father was such a likeable boy.'

'Nick is a likeable boy!' Mrs Bailey insisted. 'And he has talent!'

'Then he's hiding it under a bushel,' Mr Grange said. 'Now Chris . . .'

The bell went, then, for the end of break and the school was thronging the corridors and making for period four when the fire alarm went off, its high pitched 'whoop-whoop' resounding through the building.

Strangely enough, and despite the numbers milling about, the mass exodus was accomplished in less than three minutes and the whole school was lined up in forms and being checked when the alarm stopped.

There wasn't a fire, of course, but the fire engines came anyway, two of them, plus a flotilla of police cars.

School alarms are wired to alert the services and once activated, the system has to be carried through.

The headmaster was livid! Apart from the disruption, there was the cost to consider. Calling fire brigades out is expensive.

He paced back and forth between the class rows, pausing now and then at the group of non-form teachers who congregated by the Sports Hall for checking. The group, including Mrs Bailey, was right next to Chris's form line and, as he was at the front, he was well within earshot.

'A deliberate disruption!' he heard the Head say. 'One of the alarm points in the Arts Block . . . the glass smashed deliberately.'

'Are you sure? They swing round with those great bags on their shoulders and . . .'

'Deliberate!' the Head insisted. 'The box is tucked into a corner, by the Media Studies Suite, it couldn't have been accidental.'

It was the slightest of movements but Chris spotted it. Mrs Bailey's eyes swivelled, ran down 10C's line, stopped at Nick for a split second then swivelled back.

Chris felt the blood rising to his face as Nick grinned, winked and gave himself another stripe on his jacket sleeve.

At lunch-time, Nick's classmates were busy congratulating him on providing a respite from lessons, even if it *was* only ten minutes, but Chris was furious.

'Do you know how much it costs to call the fire brigade out?' he growled at Nick.

They were in the Quad for the ten minutes between registration and afternoon school.

'Do you know you're a prat?' Nick mocked, causing a few sniggers from his 'hangers on'.

'There's no talking to you when you're totally bonkers!' Chris said, starting to walk away, but Nick caught his arm and swung him round.

'Who asked you to talk to me and what makes you so sure it was me that did it?' he said, squaring up to impress the sniggering group behind him.

'Who else is that warped?' Chris said, shrugging away. 'You want your head testing.'

'And yours wants thumping!' Nick said, clenching his fists.

The small crowd edged away as the brothers faced each other, like two prize fighters waiting for the bell. The tension was tangible.

They had just begun to circle each other – with menace – when the crowd dispersed and they were left in the Quad with a lone observer . . . Mr Liversedge.

'What's this all about?' he asked, after a long silence.

Nick raised both hands, as though in surrender, and backed off to lean against the nearest pillar, hands in pockets and smiling.

'Chris?' Mr Liversedge said, turning to the older brother.

'Why me?' Chris cried. 'Why don't you ask him?'

'Because I'm more likely to get a straight answer from you,' the teacher said, not unkindly.

Chris was very thoughtful, for what seemed like an age, and all the time Old Liverish's eyes were fixed on him, steadily. He'd always had a good relationship with the elderly and very senior teacher . . . ever since an early encounter with Beasley and his like and Mr Liversedge had stopped the taunts and bullying. They'd had a long talk about race and religion and the persecutions that ensued from intolerance and inherited hatred and distrust. Chris had got a lot out of the talk at the time, and always made a point of speaking to Mr Liversedge, when he could. Right now he didn't quite know *what* to say.

'He's done something really stupid,' Chris said, after taking a deep breath. 'But he doesn't see it. All he sees is a chance to score a point, whatever trouble it causes for other people. He does my head in!'

'Ditto!' Nick snapped. 'I suppose you *never* do anything stupid.'

'Nothing so infantile!'

'Who're you calling an infant?'

'If the cap fits!'

'Chill out, Bro.'

'Stupid hothead!'

'Get a life, Chris. You're boring me.'

'Come here and say that!'

'Thanks for the invite.'

'*Hold it!*'

Both boys froze as Mr Liversedge raised his voice. It wasn't something he did a lot of. The RE teacher commanded quite a bit of respect from *all* the older pupils at Cannongate High. Old Liverish, so called because of his parchment coloured skin – a relic of his long years in an African mission school – had never been known to say an unkind word, make cryptic comments like some teachers did as a matter of course or treat anybody with anything but fairness and respect for individual beliefs and feelings.

He was liked and respected by staff and pupils alike and was, in Nick's eyes, what being a Christian was all about . . . caring concern for others. Nick was sure that Old Liverish was totally incapable of an unkind thought or deed. Nick admired Mr Liversedge quite a lot, though he didn't always manage to follow his example. He did try!

37

The elderly teacher had picked up one of the large pebbles that filled a decorative space between the paving slabs. He was holding it out and smiling.

' "If any one of you is without sin, let him be the first to throw a stone . . .",' he said quietly.

Nick grinned and Chris blushed, turning away as the bell went for afternoon school.

Mr Liversedge replaced the stone, nodded and hurried off to his classroom.

'OK, it was a daft thing to do,' Nick said.

Chris turned back to face him. If he'd been smiling or had acknowledged Nick's admittance, the matter might have ended right there and then. But he wasn't and he didn't. Chris was angry with himself for looking a fool in front of the teacher, an admired teacher at that, and he took it out on Nick.

'Prat!' he spat out. 'I'll get you yet!'

Nick watched him leave the Quad, sighed then cleaned the white-board with the duster that hung beside it. The marker dangled on a piece of string and Nick studied its point before he wrote two words.

Three – Nil.

The battle was still on.

They ignored each other on the bus. Chris sat on his own, obviously deep in thought, while Nick chatted up a pair of girls from the all girls' school on Hunningley Lane. One of them was a blonde.

Despite his reputation for smooth-talking the birds out of their nests, Nick was usually polite and pleasant with it – when he wasn't being watched and didn't need to augment his macho 'I'm the greatest' image. Then he would probably leer and say, 'I'm yours and isn't it your lucky day?' or something to that effect. Unobserved he was quite ordinary in his approach.

'Hi!' he said, with a devastatingly charming smile.

The fair girl pulled a face at her companion then put on a sickly-sweet grin that was more of a grimace than a smile.

'Nick Barrat,' he said, holding out his hand and ignoring her attempt at visual sarcasm. She took it, limply, and the dark girl giggled inanely.

'You're from St Margaret's,' Nick went on, nodding towards their blazer badges and wondering why he bothered with such encounters. A matter of habit, he supposed. 'I haven't noticed you two on the bus before.'

'We usually catch a later bus, but we got out early . . . just in the *nick* of time!' the blonde said, collapsing against her friend in a fit of giggles.

'Ah,' Nick said, ignoring the play on words he'd heard so many times before. 'There's a tournament at St Kentigern's on Friday – table tennis. Fancy coming along? I play doubles!'

The two girls looked at each other then back at Nick.

'All by yourself?' the dark girl said.

'With a bat in each hand?' the other added, pulling a face at her friend.

'I'm versatile,' Nick said, with a grin. 'And I've got a brother up front. Hang on!'

He left the girls, whispering together, and lurched down the cornering bus to drop into the empty seat next to Chris.

'Two tasty chicks back there,' he said, forgetting the feud. 'Mine's the blonde!'

'In your dreams, Nicholas!' Chris growled.

'Come on, Chris – they won't split up.'

'What's your problem? Can't you handle two at once?

Losing your style, brother?'

'It's only the Friendship Centre, Chris. It won't cost you anything!'

'No chance. I'm going there to win, not woo!'

'I'll stump up for Coke and crisps, it'll be a laugh!' Nick insisted, glancing back at the girls and grinning. 'Just have a look!'

Chris ignored him.

'What do you expect me to do, go back and say you don't fancy her? I'll look a right dork!'

'No more than usual,' Chris muttered, lurching to his feet and pushing past Nick. 'I'm getting off here.'

Nick followed. It was either that or humiliation.

'Thanks a bundle,' he said, once they were on the pavement and the bus had gone. 'I'll not be able to get the bus again, in case they're on it!'

'Great! I'll get some peace . . . at last,' Chris sneered, stepping into a phone box and pulling the door shut.

Nick walked on, grumbling about the extra four hundred yards between where they were now and their usual stop. He slowed down when he reached the row of shops, though, and was reading the notices on the board outside St Kentigern's when Chris caught up with him.

'Charming!' Nick groaned. 'It's St Margaret's we're playing in the tournament. What if those two turn up?'

'You'll be paying for Coke all night, turnip-head. Serves you right!' Chris sneered.

'Who were you phoning?' Nick asked, turning to look at him.

'None of your business, banana brain!'

'Not a *girlie*!' Nick mocked. 'Our Chrissy hasn't got himself a secret girlie has he? Oh joy!'

'I might have,' Chris said, with a little smile, 'but you

can keep your nose out!'

'Fear not, brother, you don't have my taste. But I can get *any* girl, including yours, if I want to.'

'You think you're really something, don't you Nick? Well, get ready to take a back seat. I'm gonna get more stripes than you've had hot dates – so don't blink, brother.'

'In your dreams, Christopher!' Nick snorted, mimicking Chris as he opened their garden gate.

Mrs Barrat was in the kitchen, ironing.

'You're late,' she said without looking at them because the collar of Mr Barrat's best shirt needed her full attention.

'Only a bit. We got off at the stop before church to check the notice-board,' Nick said, winking at Chris as if to say, 'I'm keeping your girl a secret.'

'It's the tournament on Friday night, Mum. I'll need my black T-shirt,' Chris said, scowling at Nick.

The scowl and the wink went unnoticed.

'It's upstairs on your bed, with those grey jersey joggers,' Mrs Barrat said, without looking up from the ironing-board. 'You didn't tell me what you'd be needing, Nick!'

'Best shirt, Mum. The one with the monogram. It's in my wardrobe,' Nick answered, poking about in the fridge for something to nibble.

'Aren't you playing?' Mrs Barrat said, looking up and finally satisfied with the job in hand.

'Him? Playing?' Chris gave a derogatory snort. 'We want to win, Mum, not *throw* the match away. He didn't make the team!'

'I didn't *want* to make the team,' Nick said, munching on a tomato. 'Sweating over a ping-pong ball isn't my scene. It messes up my hair!'

'But you *are* going?' Mrs Barrat asked, unplugging the iron and folding up the board.

'He was . . . until he found out that two long-nailed females will be wanting to scratch his eyes out,' Chris laughed.

'I'm going, if only to see you come a cropper!' Nick said, heading upstairs.

Usually, the family waited for Mr Barrat to get home before they had tea. It was a ritual they tried to maintain, even though the boys had things to do as they got older and their dad worked longer and longer hours as his motor repair business improved. To keep tea-time special and a family affair, Mr Barrat started work earlier. Many of the boys' friends ate meals in front of the TV, their eyes glued to *Star Trek* or one of the American sit-coms that were on at tea-time. Not the Barrat household! The family ate at the table, together, and thanked God for their health and food before they began.

Both boys accepted this as they did the regular visits to St Kentigern's on Sunday mornings and Christian Fellowship night on Tuesdays. It was part of belonging to the community – the family – of the church. Both boys had been in the choir, while still trebles, and Nick had continued to add his developing baritone when Chris, alternating between falsetto and growl, had resigned. Both considered themselves to be Christians but found it difficult to admit, out in the big bad world . . . and especially difficult with each other.

When six o'clock arrived and Mr Barrat hadn't appeared, Nick wandered into the kitchen.

'Dad's late,' he said. 'Has he got a special job on?'

'I don't think so,' Mrs Barrat said, glancing at the kitchen clock. 'But I think you'd better have yours before the whole lot dries up!'

Nick and Chris ate their casserole in the kitchen in an uncompanionable silence, then Chris settled down to his homework at the dining-room table while Nick went back upstairs, ostensibly to tidy his room.

'No homework?' Mrs Barrat had said. 'Then upstairs with you and do something with that bomb-site you call a bedroom!'

It was almost nine when a tired, angry and ravenous Mr Barrat staggered into the kitchen and slammed the back door. Nick was in the lounge watching TV and Chris was still in the dining-room but their dad's voice brought them both to the kitchen where Mum was trying to recover some of the evening meal and make it palatable.

'Unbelievable!' Mr Barrat cried, banging his fists on the table as he sat down. 'Four hours they were at it, turning everything upside down and poking into every nook and cranny!'

'What's wrong?' Nick asked, joining his father at the table. 'What's happened?'

Chris stayed by the hall door, quiet for once, but nobody noticed – not then.

'The police turned up about half past four,' Mr Barrat sighed, turning his food over with his fork. 'They wouldn't say what it was all about but they took my name and address, and the lads' too.

' "What's up?" I asked them, but you know the routine . . .

' "Just conducting a few enquiries," they said.

'Enquiries? They turned the garage upside down! Tools, motors – they were into everything. *Then* they wanted to see the office. *My* office! They went through it with a fine-tooth comb!

' "Where did you buy this car? Whose motor is that?

When did you acquire this?"

' "What are you looking for?" I ask them, but they say nothing till half an hour ago. Then because they've found nothing suspicious – everything above board and tickerty-boo, they apologise and let on they'd had a phone call!'

'A phone call?' Mrs Barrat echoed. 'What do you mean, a phone call?'

Nick had a funny feeling that he knew exactly what he meant *and* what kind of phone call it was. He glanced at Chris, who was still at the door but looked a little pale.

'Some joker tipped them off that I was running a stolen car racket. At *my* garage!'

'But you've never done anything like that!' Mrs Barrat said, as white as a sheet.

'You know it and I know it, but the police didn't. They were sorry when they found nothing – apologised for wasting my time – and they weren't too pleased at wasting *their* time either! I'm so relieved, Brenda, I feel like laughing, except it isn't funny!'

'Do you know who made the call?' Chris asked from the doorway, his voice little more than a whisper. He was already backing towards the stairs and bolted up them as Nick got up.

'Anonymous . . .' Mr Barrat said, accepting a ham and tomato sandwich in lieu of the ruined casserole, but Nick didn't wait to hear any more. He was upstairs and pushing at the bedroom door before Chris had time to close it.

'You prat!' Nick growled, pushing Chris face down on the bed and kneeling on him.

'Get off!' Chris mumbled, his face pressed down into the duvet.

There was a silent struggle until both boys fell off the bed with a muffled thump; the duvet, they had become tangled in, breaking their fall.

'It's the sort of thing *you* do!' Chris gasped, fending off Nick's blows.

'Not to my own dad I don't, you idiot. Your own dad!'

'It was a joke!' Chris insisted in a moment's respite while Nick got his breath back. 'And it's worth more than one stripe, brother . . . three at least! You've never done *anything* that big!'

Nick shook his head in disgust and turned away. 'I wouldn't want to,' he said.

'You'd better not let on!' Chris cried, going after Nick and dragging him round by the shoulder. 'It's your fault, anyway!'

'My fault?' Nick said, gathering up the front of Chris's jersey and almost lifting him off his feet. 'Why is it my fault?'

'You're always trying to be top dog. You needed teaching a lesson!'

'I needed teaching a lesson?' Nick laughed. 'I should ram your stupid words down your stupid throat!'

'Get off, Nick. Get off! I shouldn't have . . . but you send me mental. I didn't think and I wished I hadn't as soon as I put the phone down. Gerroff Nick, I'm choking!'

'You'll wish you hadn't for a long time,' Nick said menacingly. 'You're out of order this time, Chris!'

As Nick spoke and Chris almost gasped his last, the bedroom door opened and Mr Barrat pulled them apart.

'What's this then? It's not like you two to be fighting,' he said angrily. 'I know it's not the first time and you'll always have your little differences, so it probably won't be the last, but there's no need for this! You're brothers, and you should—'

'He's not my brother!'

Nick heard himself say it as his mother appeared. Her faced paled, his dad took a step backwards and Chris collapsed, breathless, on the bed.

Nick could have bitten off his tongue but it was too late. The words had been said.

~ 4 ~

Nick

So we have a conference!

It's all *my* fault of course, which is charming, seeing that it's Chris's idiotic action that started the fireworks. He needed punching for doing what he did.

I suppose I could spill the beans and drop him in it, point out that the nerd phoned the police as some sort of twisted joke, but the fat would really be in the fire if I did.

Instead, it's me that's at fault for making one small remark . . . which was the truth, anyway!

I know all about loving your neighbour and us being brothers as Christians, but it's hard, faced with someone like Chris.

I make promises to God. I guess everybody does. I pray for help to be what I know I should be but I *still* step out of line.

Last Sunday's reading suddenly jabs my mind – the Parable of the Unforgiving Servant and the last line . . . 'That is how my Father in heaven will treat every one of you unless you forgive your brother from your heart.'

It pulls you up sharp, that, doesn't it?

Nobody's saying anything and Mum's standing there, all white-faced and hurt-looking and the silence is awful – so awful I have to fill it with something, which I suppose will have to be an apology.

'I didn't mean to say it,' I mumble, looking at my feet because her eyes are so blue and wet-looking that they make me feel hollow inside. I wonder if Chris is feeling anything?

'Tell us another one!' he scoffs, and for two pins I'd smash him on the nose. That's how it is, you see. Every time I'm filled with good intentions and mean to bury the hatchet (and *not* in the back of his head!), the dork says or does the wrong thing. He really winds me up.

I must look as if I'm going to thump him because Mum steps in. 'I don't want any more of it!' she says, wringing her hands. 'I want it sorting, right now!'

Chris slumps on to the nearest kitchen stool and Mum's looking at *me* for answers.

Why me?

'What were you fighting about?' she asks, and she's not going to give up until she gets an answer she can live with. 'I know you have your little differences but it must be serious to make you fight, so who's going to tell me what's the matter?' she goes on, settling in for a long wait – and it's *me* she's looking at, again.

'Ask Chris!' I say, sharply.

'I'm asking you,' she says, hands on hips.

'That's a change, it's usually me,' Chris mutters.

'I'll talk to you next,' Mum says. 'Nicholas?'

Now *that's* one for the book! I'm never 'Nicholas' to Mum. Nicky, Nick-Nack, Nico – yes . . . when she's feeling really affectionate – but Nicholas? Lead me to the doghouse!

'We had a difference of opinion,' I say, trying to ease out of a difficult situation. Much as I detest the prat, I can't drop him in it. Not this time.

'What about?' Mum says, not to be fobbed off, and I glance at Chris.

He's gone green at the gills and his eyes are flicking shiftily. Some help *he* is, and he's the stupid one!

'About a girl,' I say, suddenly inspired. 'We were fighting over the same girl.'

Mum relaxes, visibly, and I feel the tension easing, just a bit.

'A girl!' she says, nodding. 'I thought as much.'

It was as easy as that and Chris the Culprit is allowed to go and I'm kept back to talk about this 'brother' thing.

It's hard to explain but I try, anyway.

'I know he's my brother and we should "stick together against the world" and all that sort of thing, but sometimes he's stupid and I get so mad I say things I don't mean,' I say, with feeling.

I mean it too, honest! We all say things we shouldn't, and wouldn't, if we thought before we opened our mouths. It's a spur of the moment thing and out before we know it. I've heard loads of kids say they hate their dads, can't stand their fussing mums and detest their siblings.

Nice word that, siblings. Makes me think of swans . . . no, they're cygnets!

Anyway . . . I'm no different from anybody else, except I'm better looking. And I can think of dozens of things people say, that they don't mean: 'I could kill him,' 'I could wring his neck' and 'never darken my door again!'

And what about 'I could murder a drink?' There's a concept to conjure with!

So I denied my brother? I haven't fingers enough to count the times he's denied me.

Anyway, Mum seems satisfied that we've quarrelled over some wonderful female and leaves us to get on with sorting it out amicably, after giving us a breakfast lecture (accompanied by the crunching of cornflakes) about caring Christian attitudes, which we both know about and believe in, except when we disagree.

On the bus, I have a serious think. Typically, Chris takes the only seat so I prop myself up near the front, taking care not to obstruct the driver – for which misdemeanour one is likely to be thrown off and it's raining

Standing there, shifting my weight as the bus rolls and corners, I remember the talk we had, one Fellowship night. The speaker – a Salvation Army captain who'd just come back from Sarajevo – told us how, as a young man, he'd come upon a terrible accident and had watched while the emergency services, two men in uniform, had risked their lives to get the victims out of the wrecked and burning cars. The speaker wondered if he would help, if the same thing happened today, or would he be more inclined to take off his uniform and mingle with the crowd to avoid the danger and the distress? He hoped he wouldn't.

The whole point of the story was that some Christians are like chameleons – lizards with the power to change their colour according to their surroundings. Supposedly, an experiment was carried out on a chameleon. It was put on a tartan background, couldn't take the strain of trying to be every colour and exploded!

Chameleon Christians merge with their surroundings; happy to be Christians in the company of other Christians but hide their commitment to Jesus . . . change their colours – their standards – when it isn't convenient.

I can almost hear the speaker's voice, telling us that Christians are not called to fit in with their background but to be different, to remain distinctive, to retain their Christian identity, to wear their uniform of the Christian faith for all to see and recognise.

Suddenly I feel great . . . I understand!

I catch Chris's eye and I grin. He looks surprised.

As Christians we're asked to love our brothers, our neighbours and our enemies and it's no good talking about it, we have to let it be seen, show it.

So I try. I show it!

'Want me to carry that?' I ask as Chris gets off the bus. He has his school bag, full, his sports bag, full, and a carrier bag (full!) of library books.

His eyes pop out on stalks. 'What's with you?' he says, but he hands me the carrier bag, the heaviest!

'Let's just say I've had a talk with myself . . . and a friend,' I tell him.

'Truce?' he says, and I nod. 'Thanks for keeping it dark, about the phone call,' he adds.

'It was a daft thing to do, Chris.'

'I know,' he nods. 'I'm an idiot.'

I don't contradict him.

'Sorry about the "brother" episode,' I mumble.

'It's OK,' he says. 'I feel the same way about you, sometimes.'

We arrive at school and the lack of aggro gets the day off to a reasonable start. I don't cross any of the teachers and manage to please at least two of them.

Tea-time is a pleasant affair. Dad's home early and seems to have got over his upset, deciding it was just a kid having a lark (he couldn't be more right). He thinks it might have been a good thing, in the end, because the garage has never been so tidy and organised – now that the lads have sorted and tidied the mess and disturbance the police left behind.

'I've found that set of plug spanners my dad left me,' he says, rubbing his hands together with pleasure at something forgotten and restored.

I feel that something has been forgotten and restored, too!

Mum is beaming because me and Chris are communicating like brothers should, and laughing about the funny things that happen in school. Like this afternoon when Tubby Tonkins smashed a chair, just by sitting on it, and old man Potter fell asleep half-way through a lesson and everybody left the classroom, very quietly.

After tea, we both get togged up for Youth club and the Tournament – Chris in sports gear, out for glory and me, suave and handsome, out to impress some unsuspecting chick. They can't resist me when I'm wearing my best smile!

Dad's off to night school, where he's making a stained glass panel for the front door, so he offers to drop us off. It's a great help because there's a bit of a wind springing up and I hate roughed-up hair . . . when it's mine.

I look cool, man. Cool!

Chris *looks* the sporty type and starts running on the spot as soon as we hit the hall adjoining St Kentigern's Church.

It isn't an old church, St Ken's. It's on the site of an older building that got bombed in the war and was rebuilt in the fifties, when Dad was a lad. It's red brick and glass and fairly modern in design but it's got atmosphere. It could be the cellars, part of the old crypt, where we keep our bits of scenery and the staging for our concerts, but I think it's the memories left behind from the old times. There are still old gravestones in the grounds and the site has a history . . . Roundheads and Cavaliers and all that. It might be a modern building but, inside, it has that feeling of peace and hushed anticipation that cathedrals have. It makes you want to whisper so as not to disturb the peace. The funny thing is, that we sing such great hymns – new ones with great tunes that our organist brought with him – and then the place is full of the noise of drums, tambourines and guitars. It's great!

It might seem stupid not to have restored the old stone church but, looking at its surroundings, right on the edge of a huge red-brick housing estate, it fits in, very well, with the community as it is now. You see? I do have sensible and profound thoughts.

The Fellowship Hall is an even newer building – hard earned by the community over X number of years and worth every hour of the sponsored walks, swims, climbs, sings and silences we've all put in. It has several small meeting rooms, a concert hall with a fabulous stage, a small social area with seats and tables and a kitchen/café that Mrs Sanderson opens on Fellowship and Youth nights and, of course, for refreshments when we have a show.

She's quite young, like the Reverend Sanderson himself – who's a trendy vicar and likes us to call him Jeremy. Mum and Dad, old-fashioned, stick to Mr Sanderson, though. But most of us – the boys that is – prefer to call him The Rev. It fits.

The girls call him Jeremy. I suppose they fancy him,

or fancy the *idea* of him, if he wasn't married. He's not bad, in a palely poetic sort of way, but I'm better looking.

Anyway . . . Chris is running on the spot, limbering up he says, and I take a quick scan over the talent. Not the *teams* you understand. The team *followers*.

There's nothing worth the effort of making myself look debonair, as yet!

There's no sign of the girls from the bus and I suppose that's reasonable. The opposing team's from St Margaret's Church Youth Group and not from the adjoining girls' school. There's not a dolly worth drooling over in the place. What a drag.

I'm just consoling myself with a Coke and a choccy biscuit when 'She' walks in.

You know how it is . . . you hear Meatloaf singing 'I would do anything for love,' and although she isn't exactly a 'Lady in Red' she's got red hair.

WOW KERPOW!!

She's it! 'The' one, and the drooling begins.

Trouble is, she's in the opposing team and out of bounds to onlookers like me. Why didn't I make an effort and play the game? They even have squash delivered at half-time!

At one point, I have a leg over the rope barrier that separates *watchers* from *players*, my hand on my heart and the gleam of the chase in my eye when The Rev puts a restraining hand on my arm.

'Down, boy,' he says, grinning.

I back off, for the moment.

Anyway, from afar I continue to watch the play – the ping-pong *and* my brother's futile attempt at pulling the object of my breathless gaze, the fascinating redhead in the little white shorts.

I know we've declared a truce, Chris and me. But this is serious stuff. She's mine, brother . . . mine, and isn't all fair in love and war? I won't punch him; honest. I'll gently ease myself into her consciousness and kick him out of touch with a marshmallow boot. No fisticuffs – promise!

It's like watching *Neighbours*!

First, Chris plays against a nerd and his victory's a cinch. Game over, he goes and chats up the girlie and she's taking it on board – I can tell her. Her eyes have gone all soft and fluttery and she's twiddling her flaming pony-tail. Scrumptious!

Chris wipes the floor with opponent number two and is well on the way to the final without much effort. It grieves me to admit it, but he's good, our Chris. He asks a lot of himself but he always comes up to scratch. He's a sportsman, no doubt about it and I'm one to give the credit, where it's due. (Big of me that, isn't it?)

Anyway, there's a refreshment break before the second half and the doubles matches. The heats were played last week for those, so there's only the semi and the finals to play.

I see an opening and make for the café, to grab two Cokes before the rush. Then, a bottle in either hand – better than a can and a lot more trendy – and looking like *I* do, the redhead hasn't a chance.

Neither have I! The Rev steps in front of me and places a hand on my chest to stop me edging past. He wants something; I know it and, just now, I haven't a moment to spare, or a hand. Chris is already buying drinks!

'Nick,' The Rev says. 'I wonder if you'll do me a service?'

What can I say? He's a nice guy and I can hardly ask

him what sort of service it is, as though it makes a difference.

He beckons – with the hand that isn't preventing my escape, and we're joined by a double dose of junior jollity. Two little girls, alike as two peas in the proverbial pod and both open-mouthed and expectant.

'These are my nieces, Bethany and Leah,' The Rev goes on. 'They're over from Australia, visiting Grandma, and are staying with us for the weekend. They demanded to watch the tournament. Exciting, isn't it girls?'

They nod, in unison, and out of the corner of my eye I see Chris – the girl of my dreams in tow and both hands full of Coke – making for a secluded table away from my prying eyes.

'Will you look after them while I help Laura?' The Rev goes on, nodding towards Mrs Rev who's having a hard time dealing with the thirsty rabble.

What can I do?

What can I say?

The Rev has made a request and I can't refuse. He's a great guy and has made a tremendous difference at St Kentigern's. The congregation's doubled since he took over and the Fellowship's really thriving. He's got that 'glow' about him that makes you want to smile and he's full of ideas for getting the community into church, especially the kids. I think he's great so I smile and nod. It hurts – but I nod.

'Come and have a Coke,' I say, with a forced smile and my left eye on Chris and the girl. I'm still holding the two I've bought so we don't need to queue up and I lead The Rev's sproglettes to the nearest empty table.

They look about six, or eight. Who can tell? One of them has a red birthmark, about an inch long, on her left temple, and apart from that I'm seeing double!

'Which one's Bethany?' I ask.

'Me,' the one with the birthmark says 'And I'm the oldest.'

So *that's* sorted out!

Conversation over and not really interested in watching them suck their drinks through a straw – noisily and in unison – I let my eyes wander over the gathering. Our chaps are chatting up the girls from St Margaret's and getting closely acquainted, and our females (not that any of them are what you might call tasty and worthy of my attention) are fluttering their eyelashes at the opposing team talent . . . and not of the ping-pong playing sort.

There's Carrie Anders, doling out drinks with Mrs Rev, but she's a friend – not a date, *and* she's chatting with Gaz and getting on fine by the look of it.

And what am I doing? Nick Barrat, Casanova of Cannongate, is entertaining a pair of Munchkins from Oz! Wizard!

The mixed doubles progress to their logical conclusion, with our top team winning, as usual. Rick Denton and Sophie Warner are an unbeatable pair, when they're on form and tonight they are just that.

Chris never plays doubles. Come to think of it, he's never been one for sharing the glory. He runs alone, jumps alone and plays games like tennis, squash and ping-pong – alone. I know cricket's a team game and he likes that, but he prefers the bat in his hand or the ball in his fist – always Captain and out on his own. Never the fielder, he plays for himself, does Chris.

At about ten to nine, The Rev takes my encumbrances away and delivers them to Mrs Sanderson for disposal. (Home to bed, not – *disposal*!)

Chris has had a good night while I've been playing

child-minder and now it's my turn to display my prowess. He's starting another game, crouched at one end of the table, his bat at the ready and his eyes glued to the little white spheroid in his opponent's hand. How tense!

In the still, expectant silence I approach the unsuspecting prey. She's watching Chris, her little pink tongue on her top lip as she waits for his first shot.

I blow on the back of her neck. It's a winner – never fails.

She blushes, goes all weak at the knees and leans on me.

'I've been watching you all night,' I whisper.

She smiles, still staring at Chris, who is playing like an idiot and trying to watch me and the ball at the same time.

It's not *my* fault he loses the heat – and the girl. If he can't keep his mind on the game, he shouldn't play. He should set his sights and be single-minded, like me.

He isn't happy when Mick Lever pulls it off, on table two, and wins the tournament. At least the cup stays at St Ken's, no thanks to Chris!

I make for the door while he receives a trophy for winning the most games, if not the final, and he's barking mad. I can see the steam coming out of his ears! Can't think why, a trophy's a trophy, isn't it?

'Prat!' he spits out, catching me up.

'What did *I* do?' I ask, innocently.

'You know, all right,' he says. 'I was getting on fine until you stuck your big nose in!'

'What, in the game?' I ask, not taking him up on it, but filing away that allusion to my 'big nose' for another occasion.

'No, with Stephanie!' he says.

'Stephanie! Is that her name?'

'Didn't you bother to find out?'

'Not that interested,' I reply, with a grin, and make for the gate.

Suddenly, there's a hand on my arm. It's Stephanie the redhead.

I look at her and she melts. Is it worth the effort, I ponder?

'Ah ya buyin' us sum chips, then?' she says. 'Ahm stahvin'.'

Not likely! I vault the wall, no mean feat, and leg it up Souter's Alley as fast as Chris in a crisis!

He catches me up in our avenue.

'You didn't want to go out with her anyway,' he says, panting. 'Why lead her on? I was doing all right before you stuck your . . .'

'Watch it,' I warn. If he alludes to the size of my nose again, I'll have to thump him! 'You didn't fancy her did you?' I add, feigning horror.

'Why not? She's nice-looking,' he says.

'Until she opens her mouth. Didn't you hear her talk? No, I don't suppose she got a word in, with you telling her how great you are!'

'Listen who's talking,' he says, and we're facing each other, battle stance, when mother comes out of next door.

We back off and smile.

'Hi, Mum,' I say, cheerfully. 'Been neighbouring?'

'No, I popped over to see Mrs Jeffels an hour ago and locked myself out. I hope one of you has a key. Dad's out collecting unpaid bills.'

Neither of us has a key!

'I'll get in,' says Mr Fixit, Chris, after he's had a quick look round the back. 'The bathroom window's open.'

Like Spiderman himself, Christopher shins up the fall

pipe, negotiates the gap between it and the bathroom window-sill – by edging along the half-inch protrusion of bricks that separate the lower half of the house from the pebble-dashed upper floor – and disappears, head first, through the open flap at the top of the window.

Sensational! I couldn't have done it. I'm too big, too uncoordinated and too chicken!

'My hero!' Mum cries when he opens the back door, and she gets hold of his ears, tilts his head and kisses it.

He may be *her* hero, but I'm quick to point out, when we're alone, that the only female Chris impresses is his mother!

Truce over . . . the battle resumes but no more stupid pranks on my part. From now on it's legit . . . serious stuff!

~ 5 ~

Chris

Would you believe it?

It's now become common knowledge that there's open warfare between me and Nick and at least two-thirds of the inmates of Cannongate High are looking on and cheering their chosen champion – and that doesn't include the teaching staff. I suspect *they're* with it one hundred percent!

I have *my* supporters, mostly eggheads, but Nick seems to have all the good-looking girls on *his* bench. Talk about cheer-leaders – they'll be doing dance routines to 'Hail to the Chief' in short skirts and pompoms next!

I suppose, now we've publicly acknowledged our rivalry, that it's taken on a more constrained note. We've done with pranks and scams, put away childish things and are competing in recognised theatres of war – the three 'A's – Athletics, Art and all other things Academic. The subject teachers are watching with interest and I suspect one or two of them are taking bets!

Only this morning I'm approached by Fantastic Fowler – our very fit phys ed fanatic – and informed that Nick has just put the shot further than anyone in the history of the school. Well, bully for him, old boy, bully for him!

I don't mind being *told* he's good at something but I can't hack the gleam of excitement in Fowler's eye. I suppose he expects me to dash out and pull ten muscles trying to go one better – which I don't intend to do. It takes beef, not brains to put the shot and I'm the brainy one, remember.

Just to explain why we're competing in athletics in March – we're outside for PE and sports clubs whenever it's fine, thanks to Astroturf and our all-weather track facilities. It's great, not having to wait for the summer term, when I'll be in the thick of exams. As it is, we've done mocks and a little open air activity is highly acceptable when the brain is buzzing and fatigued with learning.

Things haven't been too bad, on the whole. Nick seems a lot more amenable and patient, of late. He hasn't dragged me out of the bathroom in days!

I'm not saying he's my best buddy, but he is more tolerable than of late. I've caught him deep in thought, once or twice, and he grins. It makes a refreshing change.

Last Sunday, after morning service, The Rev comes up to us and thanks Nick for being so helpful. I don't know anything about this but Mum looks suitably impressed. As far as I know, all Nick did last Friday night was chase *my* girl and block it for me – and he dropped her at the end of it! The Rev goes on about personal sacrifice, in the service of others, with a twinkle in his eye as if he knows Nick was after a girl that night. Surely it's not a cause for congratulations! Then he tells him to 'keep at it', which, again, could be taken to mean 'keep chasing the girls' but I don't suppose it does!

Whatever Nick did was worthy of comment, that's for sure.

To be honest, I find it hard to imagine Nick doing anything for anybody, unless there's something in it for him. *And* it pleased Mum.

I tackle him at break, cornering him by the drama board.

'As a matter of interest,' I say, calmly and without apparent rancour. 'What exactly did you do for The Rev and what was in it for you?'

'Talk about delayed action,' he exclaims. 'That was last Friday!'

'He mentioned it on Sunday and it's only just registered,' I say, grinning as though it doesn't really matter anyway.

I expect him to come up with some tale of 'daring do' – for the benefit of Carrie Anders and another girl from Year Ten who are hanging about, as usual. He doesn't!

'Two little girls,' he says. 'The Rev's nieces. I looked after them for an hour.'

'Little? How little?' I snort.

He raises one eyebrow, like Roger Moore as James Bond, and sighs.

'About so big,' he says, holding his hand at chest height. 'Just about right for *you*, Chris.'

Carrie shakes her head at him.

'Give up, Nick,' she says. 'They're only about seven!'

'So?' Nick says, grinning infuriatingly.

I shrug and saunter off, not rising to the bait this time. I don't give him the satisfaction!

It doesn't make any sense! Nick Barrat gets all togged

up to get himself a girl then spends most of the night with The Rev's relatives? Most odd! There must have been an incentive — something in it for him!

And here's another oddity — he didn't split on me about that stupid phone call to the cop-shop and all the upset it caused. I expected him to! It was an open invitation for him to get the upper hand. I don't get why he didn't drop me right in it.

I did thank him, for not being a nark, but I didn't go overboard. There were things that should have been said and weren't — like how much of a prat I felt about playing such a low trick, and on Dad of all people.

I haven't a thing to say against our parents. They're great people, the best! Oh, I know I've beefed about Nick being the favourite, but only when we've been at each other's throats. They never take sides when it matters and have been there, for both of us, whenever we've needed them. And look at all the support they've given me! I've never had to say no to ATC weeks at training camp or outward bound trips, and Dad's always there when I'm competing in athletic meets, cheering me on. What more could I ask? Mum's just lovely and dead easy to talk to. She always understands how I feel and usually says the right thing to buck me up when I'm down.

What I did to Dad was terrible. I've asked God to forgive me and, strangely, The Rev's sermon on Sunday was right on the mark. He read the passage where Jesus heals a paralysed man by telling him his sins are forgiven and he talked about Jesus having God's authority, on earth, to forgive sins. It was almost as if it was directed just at me.

I'd like to apologise to Dad — own up and tell him how sorry I am, that I'm a wally and please will he forgive me – but I haven't the words . . . or the guts.

A wally without the wellie, that's me!

So – Nick's suddenly become the nice guy, and, as the competition is hotting up, I have to pull out all the stops to draw level.

So far I'm ahead, in the sporting field, with running, jumping and hurdling colours to show for it.

Nick put the shot, but it's 3–1 to me!

This week I've got A for maths, A for geography and an 'Excellent' A for physics. Nick has an A for drama. Another 3–1 to me.

Total score, 6–2 in my favour.

I point this out to Nick, who pulls a notebook out of his pocket and shows me names – girls' names – and dates.

'Eight!' he says, triumphantly.

'Eight what?' I scoff. 'Examples of joined-up writing? You are coming on!'

'Eight dates in one weekend,' he says. 'And seeing how you haven't been out since last Friday, that's 8–0 to me and a total score of . . . 10–6 in my favour.'

'Hang on,' I complain, grabbing the book. 'Who said dates are in the running? And more to the point, you haven't been on them all yet!'

'I've been on three . . . Zoe Sutton on Saturday afternoon, a great walk in the park; Fiona Mackay on Saturday night, a great film; and Lucy Radcliffe on Sunday . . . just great! The other five are pending. Getting them's the thing,' he grins.

'Where's the proof?' I growl.

'Ask the girls,' he says and saunters off.

Now that's not on, counting dates you haven't had yet, is it?

Anyway, Wednesday arrives and it's cricket trials, for

the first team. There's a County Schools Cup to be won and Cannongate High means to have it. I have a feeling that Nick fancies himself in white sweater and flannels and I'm proved right. He turns up at lunch-time and has a go in the nets.

Fat chance!

I'm in, natch, as a bowler and first man in – having a batting average on a par with Botham . . . for my age.

Nick gets nowhere near but he's unperturbed. I'd be devastated!

I meet him the canteen and drop my answer to his 'dial-a-date' points.

'Evens, brother,' I tell him. 'One up for the cricket and three more: certificates for aircraft recognition, top drill cadet and A1 rifle shooting.'

'No way! ATC doesn't count!' he says.

'It does, if dates do,' I reply with a grin and it's *me* that saunters off, leaving him gobsmacked!

After school there's auditions for parts in the next school production and I fancy my chances. I wouldn't bother, normally, because it's usually a boring play, but this year it's a musical and a favourite of mine. Mrs Bailey has decided we'll do *Grease*. Well, she didn't actually make the decision totally on her own. She put forward a few suggestions and Manic Maxwell – music – turned down the rest. He's not that brilliant a pianist and *Fiddler on the Roof* is just a bit beyond his capabilities I should imagine. The Head turned down *Cabaret* as being too controversial and *The King and I* got thumbs down because it's a one man show, except for the leading lady, and we haven't got anyone who's remotely like Yul Brynner! Mr Dixon's bald but he can't sing and, anyway, we like the cast to be 'all student' and not one of us is follically challenged! There's not much in it for a chorus, you see, and we like shows that can use a multitude!

Manic Maxwell's OK for playing hymns in assembly but his 'going in and coming out' music is dire at times. Most days he busks and twiddles little tunes with his right hand, but now and again he tries to perform Chopin and Brahms and makes a right hash of it. Great trumpet player though! Each to his own!

As *Grease* is mostly four chord stuff he can busk the left hand – well within his scope.

Anyway, we get to the hall and sit at the front, a big crowd of us. Mrs Bailey comes in and we have to go on stage and sing . . . alone!

The audition piece is 'Greased lightning', which is great as it's a song you have to yell, not sing and we don't have to do it all – time's limited because we have to catch the school bus home.

I don't get a look in! I get through one chorus of the song and Bailey says, 'OK, Chris . . . dance.'

'I gotta dance?' I say, paralysed.

'Dance,' she repeats. 'Danny Zukko (the leading man) has to dance.'

I freeze. Singing with my head down and my eyes glued to the score is one thing, but dance?

I take a stab at it but I'm no John Travolta. I'm OK in a shoulder to shoulder disco with flashing lights and a stomach-churning beat but, alone on our theatre-size stage, forget it!

Carrie Anders goes up next. She's not blonde, like Olivia Newton-John, but boy can she sing! She's great. She looks all sweet and pure and sings 'Hopelessly devoted to you' as if she means every word. She's as good as anybody I've heard sing it and she made *me* have an emotional lump in my throat – not that I'd admit to it! There's nobody to touch her.

Then it's Nick turn to strut his stuff and doesn't he just! He sings, he dances and even manages to look like a blond Travolta. He's obviously worked on the audition pieces and there's nobody to touch *him* either – so it's Nick and Carrie for the leading parts, has to be.

I could spit!

It isn't jealousy, honest. I didn't expect to get the lead in the first place and I'm quite happy being one of the chorus lads with a couple of lines to say.

It's great fun, doing a show and even if I hadn't got in the chorus I'd be there backstage.

It isn't the fact that it's another stripe on his sleeve, either! It's the strutting and the head tossing he'll be doing from now on that makes me feel sick. He's big-headed enough!

I walk to the bus with Carrie. Nothing's official, of course, but Nick's back there, 'greasing' round Mrs Bailey to make doubly sure he gets it. I don't know why he bothers. Even I can see there's no one else in his league.

'He's good, Nick. Isn't he?' Carrie says as we saunter to the gate.

'Hummph!' I growl. I suppose she thinks I'm dawdling so I can slap him on the back when he catches up. Slap him in the mouth, more like!

I like Carrie Anders. She's OK, nice-looking and she's easy to talk to. She got the French prize last Speech Day, so she ain't no bimbo either.

'He's sure to get it, isn't he?' she goes on, her eyes shining in anticipation of acting with him. She knows she'll get the part of Sandy by the look of it.

'Hummph,' I mouth again and she gets the message loud and clear.

'You should be glad for him – he's very good!' she cries.

'Glad? I'm positively ecstatic!' I protest, hand on heart and eyes rolling.

'You're jealous,' she says, hands on hips.

'I am not!'

'You are, Chris. You're boiling because he's getting the part and you're not.'

'He hasn't got it yet,' I mutter.

'Of course he has. You *know* he has. There's nobody as good as Nick – not for *this* part.'

'I suppose you're drooling at the thought of rehearsing with him,' I snarl, and she blushes, bites her lip and glares at me!

'Don't class everybody by your own standards, Chris!' she says. 'There can be such things as friendship and mutual interest between boys and girls. And we're not just objects to be leered at and discussed in the boys' room! *Grow up!*' she says, and marches off to the bus stop.

'Hang on, Carrie!' I yell, hurrying after her. I sure hit a nerve there!

I catch her up and there's a long queue so we sit on the wall to wait.

'I'm sorry,' I tell her. 'I know you're a bit gone on him but I didn't mean to imply . . .'

'I am not!' she says, tossing her head.

' "Methinks the lady doth protest too much",' I grin, quoting Shakespeare. (I think?)

'Oh, get lost!' she snaps.

I can't win!

'I'm really sorry, Carrie. I just don't understand what he's got that turns girls weak at the knees – most girls anyway. He's a show-off, a loser, and he's thick with it!'

I go on, determined to make my point.

She looks at me, right in the eye, and the minutes tick away.

'You just don't know him at all, do you?' she says, quietly.

'Know him? I live with him, don't I? If I don't know him, who does?' I protest.

She sighs and fiddles with her bag strap. After a bit she looks me in the eye again. Very disconcerting!

'You only see what you expect to see – what he *knows* you expect of him. He plays the part well,' she says.

'How profound,' I mock. 'You'll be telling me I created him, next.'

'You did, in a way,' she says. 'You've made each other. He expects you to sneer at everything he does so he makes sure he performs to your expectations – and vice versa.'

'Rubbish!' I explode, standing up and kicking at the wall with my shoe toe. 'I'm never any different. He's the dork who doesn't know who he is, who's always putting on the style!'

'We're all several people rolled into one,' Carrie says, standing up and brushing brick dust off her uniform. 'But, even though we're different things to different people, the essential "us" shines through . . . or it should!'

'Quite the philosopher,' I mutter, standing up to face her and aware that a crowd has gathered, sensing the friction. 'So what's the essential something that shines through our Nick?'

'You *really* don't understand, do you?' she says, looking sorry because I'm missing out on something important, supposedly.

'Enlighten me,' I sneer. 'It makes my day to be put

right on something I seem to be lacking the intelligence to assimilate.' (Big word, that!)

Carrie takes a deep breath, as though she's going to deliver a final statement for the defence.

'What I'm saying is, Chris, that you're both nice people, great guys and fun to be with – on your own. You're different when you're together, and even when you're talking about each other. Do you know I've never heard Nick say an unkind word, except when you're about. It's as though someone waves a red flag as soon as you get within ten feet of each other. Why can't you be the same with him as you are with . . . me, for instance?'

'Because he's a dork with no sense of responsibility and he's only bothered when there's something in it for him.'

'That's not true, Chris. And you know it!'

'Oh yeah? He looked after two little girls for an hour. Big deal!' I mutter, the episode with The Rev coming to mind.

'What *did* he get out of it? He wasn't playing in the tournament and nobody even noticed him with them. I was thinking about that time he stopped those two junior boys from fighting and spent a whole dinner hour talking them into being friends again.'

'Only because he was being watched by Mr Stanley. It's a pity he doesn't practise what he preaches!' I retort.

'He would, given half a chance. You have to meet each other half-way, Chris – practise a little give and take instead of putting each other down at every opportunity and carrying on this stupid tit-for-tat battle.'

Carrie turns away, then, and joins the end of the queue, because the bus is due, and Nick comes up behind me.

'What're you doing chatting up my Pink Lady?' he says.

'Pink Lady' is the name given to a girl who was in Danny Zukko's gang, in the musical.

'You haven't got the part, yet,' I say, taunting him and regretting it almost immediately because I've just proved Carrie's point.

'Haven't I?' he smirks, and I feel like socking him one. Carrie's not wrong. I *do* want to hit him as soon as I see him and it probably works both ways!

'There are others in the running,' I remind him.

'Not with my talent, charisma and physique,' he says, grinning. 'Not to mention my looks. Face it, Chris. You're vertically challenged, you've two left feet and you can't sing. No chance, brother!'

'Less of the "brother" thing,' I snarl, shoving him with one hand. If *he* can deny our relationship, so can I!

'Hands off!' he warns.

'Oh yeah? You and whose army?' I parry.

'I don't need one,' he thrusts.

And he has to prove he doesn't – natch!

He comes at me like a bull at a matador. I step back, right on somebody's foot, and the resulting yell of pain brings the whole queue to the arena, plus another approaching rabble who've just finished a volleyball match.

There isn't a choice in the matter . . . the die is cast. The crowd have formed a circle, our seconds are holding our coats and the bell rings for round one – ding-dong!

We dance around for a bit, fists up, and the crowd is howling for blood. Nick socks me one on the jaw and I land a well-aimed fist in his middle. He's winded and I take the advantage when he turns away to take a few deep breaths. I leap on his back and cling on for dear

72

life . . . he can't punch me from this position. I pummel away at his kidneys and manage the odd rabbit punch before he drops to his knees and rolls over, with me underneath. In a flash he's on my chest, he's got me by the ears and he's banging my head on the deck! At least we're on the grass verge so it isn't too serious, not like it would be a foot to the left, on concrete!

I'm seeing stars and trying to dislodge him with my knees when I hear the voice. Mr Cunningham!

I lie still, watching the stars circling the red mist behind my eyes, and the weight lifts off me.

When everything clears, Old Liverish is helping me up and the Head has Nick's arm in a vice-like grip.

'Home!' he says. 'And no more of it. My office tomorrow, 9:10 am on the dot. Got it?'

We get it!

I don't look at Nick and, once off the bus and glad to be away from Carrie's sad eyes, I walk home the back way to avoid him.

He's home first because his bag's on the hall floor but there's no sign of him.

Mum's waiting, arms folded and eyes sad . . .

'Bedroom!' she says, no doubt put in the picture via a phone call from school, unless Nick's ingratiated himself already. I wouldn't put it past him.

Come to think of it, I don't exactly pull my punches if there's a chance of me coming out on top!

I suppose it will all be my fault, this time, me being the oldest.

I go upstairs without a word. I'm tired, my head aches and I want to forget I have a brother.

We're served supper in our rooms and Mum doesn't want to talk about it until we've both cooled down. I'm cool already . . . shivering with it!

I can hear Nick's Reggae Rap through the wall and I'm just about to thump on it when I think of Carrie Anders and what she said. 'You're both nice people . . . great guys . . . on your own.' Does that mean we're nerds when we're together? I suppose it does.

Something has to change, though, and pretty quick if you ask me . . . fighting hurts!

~ 6 ~

Facing Foxy . . . and feeling foolish

Mr Cunningham cleared the morning mail from his in-tray, sorting it into 'immediate' and 'later' piles before pressing his desktop buzzer.

Outside, a green light appeared above his door and Mavis nodded to the Barrat boys.

Mr Cunningham waited for the ensuing knock and ignored it, a little smile playing around the corners of his mouth. A few minutes more apprehension wouldn't do them any harm.

He drained his second cup of coffee, stretched, then composed himself for the first of a series of 'Headmaster interviews' that made up his school day.

'Come in,' he said, after a suitable pause and in his best 'I'm not to be trifled with' voice.

Sometimes, the visitor failed to hear his invitation through the solid oak door but not this time. Christopher and Nicholas Barrat glanced at Mavis, the Head's secretary, and at her nod, opened the door very slowly. It creaked.

'Come in, come in! We haven't all day!' Mr Cunning-ham said, making sure they understood, by his tone, that he wasn't prepared to be a soft touch.

Chris felt terrible. He'd avoided such confrontations, up to now, and was worried about his prefect's badge and the authority it gave him. Chris was prepared to say, and do, anything that would appease the Head and maintain the status quo.

Nick was equally contrite and anxious to diffuse the situation but it wasn't to appease the Head. Nick tried to stay away from fighting. He might talk about it, even threaten it but he didn't do it, not often anyway. Nick knew his own strength *and* the fact that *he* wouldn't be the one getting hurt. It was dangerous, was fighting.

Nick and his buddies called the head Old Foxy when he wasn't in earshot – partly as a play on the name *Cunning*-ham, and partly because he was . . . as cunning as a fox!

Mr Cunningham had a way of materialising, unexpectedly, in obscure corners of the building where something was usually going on.

Chris, always suspicious, insisted there were spies everywhere, employed by the Head to keep him informed.

Nick was more inclined to believe Old Foxy had a natural ability, a sixth sense that told him what was going on in his school.

Either way, he was always well-informed. Neither of the boys realised how much time and effort Mr Cunningham *did* put in to know his staff and his pupils, to understand their needs and to create a calm yet stimulating environment for learning and growing. He was the best sort of headmaster for a large comprehen-sive like Cannongate High. Old Foxy was quite ahead, as Heads go.

'Well?' he said at last, staring unblinkingly from Nick to Chris and back to Nick as they stood to attention in front of his desk.

'We were fighting, sir,' Nick said.

'I know that, young man. The whole school, the neighbourhood and the Cannongate bus company know that! I wouldn't be at all surprised if it made national headlines! 'Barrats brawl at bus stop', a real coup for some enterprising reporter, don't you think? Don't flatter yourselves! What *I* want to know is what it was about? What could make two brothers resort to brawling in the street like a couple of ruffians?'

Both boys were silent.

'Well?' Mr Cunningham said, again.

'It was . . . a difference of opinion, sir,' Chris said, after clearing the boulder that was blocking his throat.

'All wars are the result of differences of opinion, Christopher. Adolf Hitler thought that Poland would be a nice little addition to his Third Reich. We didn't – and that difference of opinion caused World War Two!' the Head said, raising his voice a decibel or three!

'Yes, sir,' Chris muttered.

'Yes, sir? Does that signify agreement, Chris, or are you confirming the historical correctness of my analogy?'

'I'm agreeing, sir,' Chris said, clearing his throat and relaxing a little. At least the Head had dropped the 'Christopher' which was a good sign.

'And do you have anything to say, Nicholas?'

'We'd just auditioned for the play, and Chris was—' Nick began, but was interrupted.

'Don't tell me you were brawling on the pavement – in public – because one of you got a part in a play and the other didn't?' the Head cried, sitting back in his seat.

'No, not only that,' Chris said.

'Then what, Chris – Nick? Tell me what else.'

Once started there seemed to be no stopping the Barrats as they listed their grievances. But – as they were both talking at the same time and neither could be understood in the resulting gabble – the Head stood up and banged on the table.

'Hold it,' he said sternly. 'We'll get nowhere with the pair of you gabbling like a couple of turkeys! Shut up and sit down!'

He waved his hand towards the 'visitor' end of the room, where three low chairs were arranged around a smoked glass coffee table, and, when they were seated and quiet, he took over the conversation.

'I am aware of your rivalry,' he said, calmly. 'And rivalry is no bad thing in its place and in moderation. Competition, *healthy* competition that is, never did anyone any harm. If we didn't compete, we'd lose our purpose, our incentive, wouldn't we? Some years ago a few schools abandoned it altogether – did away with House points and all competitive sports. A bad idea in my opinion. How else are we driven to try and try again to be the best we can be?'

Chris nodded. He could live with that.

Nick was thoughtful, visibly so.

'Nick?' the Head said, sensing the hesitation.

'I don't think people should make it the be-all and end-all,' Nick said. 'It's playing the game that counts, not winning it.'

'True,' the Head said, nodding. 'But isn't it also true that we perform better if there's something to gain – a place in a team, a part in a play? Don't we give of our best when there's something at the end of it? Didn't Chris practise and strive for a place in the cricket team?

78

Didn't you, Nick, throw yourself into the part to be sure you were considered for the lead? Didn't you learn the words so you could perform without the book and put together some dance steps to show you have John Travolta feet? Isn't that healthy competition, giving of your best to gain an end? It does make another point, too. Everybody can be good at something.'

Mr Cunningham paused, leaning back in his chair and pressing the tips of his fingers together. Chris and Nick relaxed a little, settling back in their chairs as they recognised the signs. Old Foxy was about to reminisce, to tell a tale as an illustration and they'd have at least a ten minute respite.

'My maternal grandmother lived in a small village in northern India, near Srinagar, where my father was based and where he met my mother. My grandmother, my *Gammoo*, was a lovely old lady, or at least she *seemed* old when I was a small boy.

'My parents and I lived in a large white house with pillars at the front and a pool. I had my own *ayah* – nurse, I suppose you'd call her here – to look after me because father was well off and quite important. We lived a very peaceful and comfortable life, while Grandmother lived in a one-roomed hut and cooked on hot bricks that surrounded the ever-burning fire that smoked the place out. She preferred to stay in her village and, do you know, on that primitive stove she made the best chapattis ever? She couldn't read, write or do anything *we* would consider a talent, but those chapattis were something else.

'We couldn't talk to each other much because, although I did learn the odd word here and there, I spent most of my childhood at school in England. Besides, she spoke a Hindi dialect far removed from anything I learnt.'

The Head seemed to be lost in some reverie of his own, and only returned to the present when Chris cleared his throat for the third time.

'What I'm saying is,' he said suddenly and turning Chris's cough into a hiccup. 'We all have something to offer – something peculiar to ourselves and that healthy competition is beneficial . . . a way of honing ourselves, developing ourselves to the full. Think of all those people who give their time and effort to raising money for people in need. I can think of a fine example – Chris Chataway! He was a runner, middle and long distance. He beat the two mile world record in 1953 – 8:49.2 and the mile relay record with Roger Bannister that same year. Athletes were all amateurs then, and didn't get the vast sums of money that are handed out these days. They did it for the love of sport and, in Chris's case, for the glory of God . . . and he wasn't afraid to confess his faith. He acted as pacemaker for Bannister when the first four minute mile was run in 1954 and *that* was a selfless act if ever there was one! Chataway became an MP in 1969 and later used his fame and good name to sponsor and help create the Action Aid scheme, where people sponsor the education and care of a child in a third world country.

The human need to compete is good when it's founded in friendship and the desire to create a happy world. It isn't healthy when it causes trouble between brothers! Don't you think it's time to live and let live, turn the other cheek, stop rising to the bait and cease this tit-for-tat tournament? Can you think of any other clichés that fit?'

When there was no answer to that, he went on. 'I think you'll find that the greatest pleasure is born out of using your talents for others.'

80

Chris glared at Nick, who glowered back.

'I know he's better at some things and I'm better at others. That's not the problem,' Chris said. 'We've always competed and it used to be fun!'

'What stopped it being fun?' Mr Cunningham asked.

'He started whingeing, running to Mum and the teachers. He hasn't got the guts to face up to criticism,' Nick sneered.

'Rubbish!' Chris cried, quick to defend himself. 'I get picked on because I'm different. With half the school chasing you, you have to complain, or it's curtains! And you're the one that started everything . . . telling stupid stories!'

'Stories?' Mr Cunningham said.

'Yeh! Telling them I'm the son of some maharajah – an heir to some pile, with millions in a secret bank! You name it, he's said it! He thought it was funny!'

'I didn't! I thought it was great. I wanted you to be special, then!' Nick protested.

'Then!' Chris said. 'It wasn't all that long before you changed your tune and started to run me down!'

'Me, run *you* down? What do *you* do?' Nick protested. 'You're always on about how thick and useless I am because I'm not an egg-head, like you!'

'What good is it, being good at things? You're the favourite at home, even though you don't get straight As. Blood's thicker than water!'

'And *that's* a load of rubbish and you know it,' Nick cried. 'You ask for everything you get. You use the "colour" thing to get your own way – you *all* do. We're expected to let things go in case we offend the . . .'

'Ethnic minority?' Mr Cunningham said, smiling.

Nick blushed, realising what he'd implied and embarrassed by his lack of thought. Mr Cunningham was

Anglo-Indian, of mixed race, and Nick wasn't sure what reaction there would be to his outburst.

Chris had a gleam in his eye, as if enjoying Nick's discomfort and the ever-discerning Old Foxy took both expressions on board.

'Chris?' he said, his tone a question.

Chris hesitated, not sure what he was meant to say next. There was a long pause while he thought about it and Nick gazed, intently, out of the window.

It was Nick who spoke first.

'Chris assumes that anybody against him, in any way, is against him because he's different. That's rubbish! I have a go at him because he acts stupid and he makes me mad! He's paranoid! He's convinced there's a conspiracy against him and I'm the leader!'

'It isn't that simple,' Chris butted in. 'You don't have to put up with it, with being different. You don't get the funny looks and the snide remarks. Nobody asks *you* where you were born!'

'I have to put up with *you*,' Nick retorted. 'And you with *me*. We're stuck with each other – for better, for worse . . . in sickness and in health!'

Mr Cunningham smiled and nodded, as if in agreement.

'You see!' Chris cried. 'You're taking his side, just like everybody does!'

'I'm not taking anybody's side, Chris. I'm just agreeing with Nick on a pertinent point. You *are* brothers and you'll have to learn to live with the fact. Beg to differ on all other points, if you must, but at least agree on that one.'

Neither of the boys protested that they weren't brothers . . . not this time.

Mr Cunningham stood up and went to look out on

his school gardens and grounds. He seemed deep in thought and Nick was just wondering if they should creep out and leave him to it when he spoke, more quietly and with his back to them.

'It took me a long time to come to terms with the differences *I* met, as a child. I spent term-time in England where, in those days, I was a bit of an oddity – me with my brown skin, black hair and my peculiar way of talking. It wasn't peculiar at all, really, just everyday standard BBC English but it sounded odd against the local dialects I encountered. Every time I forgot where I was and mentioned my *ayah* – whom I loved – or used a word like *Chupah* or tiffin, I was laughed at and pushed around. Somebody got hold of the word *Chi-Chi* which means "half-cast" so it became my nickname. I hated it.

'In the holidays, at home in Srinagar, things were little better. In my father's house and among his friends I was treated with politeness as befitted the son of an important man but, in Grandmother's village, the children looked on me with suspicion because I *wasn't* as brown as they were. I was *Chi-Chi* to them, too! I couldn't win!

'I didn't seem to fit wherever I was. I tried to be a Christian, to love my neighbour as I'd been taught, but it's hard when everybody calls you names and won't let you play with them. I don't remember having any friends, not close ones, until I was in my teens and an Indonesian prince joined my tutor group.

'His name was Ali Bin Mustamin and everybody wanted to know him, of course, but he preferred *my* company. I suppose I brought "home" a little nearer in the grey English summers. He sought my company and it was quite a change!

'I had one foot in each camp, you see, and I drifted from one to the other, throughout my childhood, without really belonging to either. It was Mr Liversedge that put me right.'

'Mr Liversedge?' Chris said, puzzled and thinking that Old Liverish must be ancient if he'd taught the Head as a boy.

'Yes. I met him at university,' Mr Cunningham went on, solving Chris's puzzle. 'He was in his final year when I was a freshman. We both lived in hall, just across the landing, and we spent many evenings together.

'He's very interested in world religions, you know, and picked my brains on the subject of 'village Hinduism'. I grew up amongst it, of course, and could tell him more about it than any textbook.

'In return, he made me aware of how Jesus can transform our lives, if we let him. I suppose we learnt from each other, that year . . . He, strong in his Christian faith, was able to study and understand Hinduism as an *expression* of belief. He showed me where there were similar beliefs. He saw that Hinduism encouraged us to care for each other.

'I realised that he had a genuine love for people he met. It wasn't like he was trying to prove that he, *himself*, was a good person. But he showed me that we can only do the right thing when Christ *transforms* our lives.

'Unlike *any* of the Hindu gods, God loved us so much that he sent his own son to die for each one of us, to save us from sin. Whoever believes in him will not die but have eternal life. So, Jesus, himself, is able and willing to forgive our mistakes if we come to him. Then he will help us to live a new life and to follow his path.

'I, myself – hanging somewhere in-between worlds and not sure which way to swing – found belief in the one true God and the love of Jesus, his son . . . and was re-born. It changed my life when I realised that Jesus loved *me* . . . Alexander Cunningham, and that his love was unconditional and not dependent on the colour of my skin or the way I formed my words. Where else but within the Christian faith would we find such love and understanding?'

He turned, then, and looked at them both intently, as if willing them to understand *him*.

'I'm not going to punish you,' he said, smiling again as both boys let out a long and thankful sigh.

Fighting usually meant exclusion for at least three days and reinstatement needed a parental visit and an assurance of exemplary behaviour for ever more!

'But I want you to work at it,' Mr Cunningham added. 'Spend some time looking at yourselves. Write down your differences and learn to appreciate them. The world would be a dull place if we were all the same. List your similarities and rejoice in them! Believe me, it's uplifting when you find something you have in common. Look at me and Old Liverish!'

The Head grinned as the boys' eyes widened at his use of *their* nickname for his friend.

'He with his Doctor of Divinity and me with a PhD – Doctor of Philosophy – as different as chalk and cheese!' he went on. 'But, what we *had* in common was a pair of inquiring minds that were searching for truth. Imagine my joy when I got this Headship and found him here, a senior and much appreciated teacher!'

The bell went, then, and Mr Cunningham realised that he'd kept the boys a full period.

'I'll be in the doghouse now,' he said. 'Make my apologies to your teachers, will you? I'll carry the can . . . this time!'

Nick, for one, realised that Old Foxy was a lot more human than he'd thought.

'Thank you, sir,' Chris muttered as they made for the door.

'One more thing!'

Chris's heart sank. Here came the crunch, the punch line! He fully expected Old Foxy to say he'd be calling their parents.

He didn't.

'Apart from your 'similarities and differences' lists – which I'd like to see, sometime in the not too distant future – I want you both to visit the RE Room after school, just for ten minutes or so. Read Matthew, chapter seven, verses one to five and write down your thoughts. You can leave them with Mr Liversedge and still be in time to catch the second bus, right?'

Nick and Chris nodded and hurried off. Then, as soon as they were back in the Quad, they faced each other in silence. Neither seemed to know what to say.

'We're missing *second* lesson, now,' Nick said at last, trying to break the ice and be cheerful in adversity.

Chris didn't say a word. He stared at Nick as though he didn't know him at all.

'What a bonus!' Nick went on. 'I needed an excuse to miss maths, I haven't done—'

'Don't you care?' Chris cried angrily. 'Doesn't it bother you that we've just shown ourselves up as stupid adolescents who can't get on with each other like normal people? I feel like crawling into a hole and you're standing there as if we've won a victory by getting off light.'

Nick gritted his teeth and clenched his fists.

'You just can't let it go, can you?' he said. 'You have to put the last word in and make *me* the villain of the piece. Of course I care, you dumb cluck! I just have a different way of showing it. I'm not laughing it off and forgetting it, as you seem to think. I'm trying to cover up how bad I feel – you let it all hang out! Aren't we supposed to be accepting our differences?'

Chris grunted some reply that Nick didn't catch then added, 'See you in Liversedge's room,' before trundling off, hands in pockets and head down.

At lunch-time the Barrat boys made a point of avoiding each other. Chris joined Gaz Cooper at his table and Nick sat alone and as far away as possible, a fact that didn't go unnoticed. But, as they rarely spent time together and had attempted to put each other in hospital the previous day, they were left well alone. No one wanted to get mixed up in *that* affair!

Carrie Anders watched them both, from her table by the door, and sighed.

'I wish they could be friends,' she said to the new girl she was showing around. 'Chris is ever so brainy and really helpful if you don't understand something. He spent ages explaining my last physics assignment – a whole lunch-hour – and he's not even in our year.'

'He's nice-looking,' Rachel Gale said, shyly.

'Not as nice as Nick,' Carrie said, nodding towards him at the opposite end of the canteen.

Rachel studied Nick then turned her attention back to Chris.

'No,' she said. 'I think Chris is better – more mature and . . . sort of . . . romantic-looking. He reminds me of that silent movie star . . . Rudolph somebody. He was my great-gran's hero. He played a film called *The Sheik*. It's a really old movie we studied in media studies last year, to show how a tiny movement, like the twitch of an eyebrow, can be *very* expressive. Valentino . . . that was his name, Rudolph Valentino.'

'I'll introduce you sometime.' Carrie grinned, rather

pleased that the very pretty new girl didn't fancy the younger Barrat, or know that it was Nick who had the expressive twitchy eyebrows!

At 3:45pm, the Barrat brothers arrived at the RE Room, still ignoring each other.

Mr Liversedge was bent over his desk, sorting through some buff folders for a set of worksheets he needed for the following day, and he looked surprised when they walked in. He straightened up and leant backwards, his hands pressed into the small of his back as if he was trying to ease a pain.

'Welcome, and to what do I owe this honour?' he asked, smiling. 'It isn't often I'm visited by *two* Barrats at the same time!'

'Mr Cunningham's sent us to read something,' Nick said. 'Some verses from Matthew.'

'Matthew seven, one to five,' Chris added. 'And we have to make notes and hand them in to you.'

'Matthew seven, is it? I see! A little imposition imposed on a pair of battling brothers! Here are two copies of the New Testament and a wad of file paper. Go to it, my lads! Did you know that detentions were called impositions at my school, when I was a boy? Impots . . . that's what we called them . . . Impots!'

Mr Liversedge wandered away, lost in his memories of 'Impots past' while Nick and Chris took seats at opposite sides of the classroom and began to read.

'Do not judge others, so that God will not judge you, for God will judge you in the same way as you judge others, and he will apply to you the same rules you apply to others. Why, then, do you look at the speck in your brother's eye and pay no attention to the log in your own eye? How dare you say to

88

your brother, "Please let me take that speck out of your eye,"
when you have a log in your own eye? You hypocrite! First
take the log out of your own eye, and then you will be able to
see clearly to take the speck out of your brother's eye.'

The two boys read, glanced at each other then scribbled on their papers. So intent were they that, even when Mr Liversedge said their ten minutes were up, neither of them stopped. The RE teacher smiled as he packed his briefcase. He didn't know what they were writing, but something seemed to have struck a chord in the Battling Brothers Barrat, something strong and important enough to make them miss the second bus and face a half-hour wait or a long walk home.

~ 7 ~

Nick

Today is the very first day of the rest of my life, and it's not just because I've taken a good, long look at myself and promised to change.

I, Nicholas Edward Barrat, am in love! She walks into the drama room this morning and into my life, for ever! Did I say walk? It doesn't describe it . . . she glides.

Her name is Rachel, Rachel Gale. I heard her telling Mrs Bailey. It sounds like the name of a romantic heroine, doesn't it? Well, she's *my* heroine and she's absolutely, fabulously gorgeous and definitely for me! Nicholas and Rachel, Rachel and Nick. Sort of goes together, don't you think?

She walks in with Carrie Anders and bells start ringing. OK, we're early out of assembly and it's the start of lesson one, but don't knock it! The bell actually rings the exact second she appears – is that real or what!

'She's just started, today,' Carrie says, grinning because she can see I'm struck dumb. 'She's in our tutor group and she's doing drama and theatre studies.'

'Hi,' I say, standing tall and raising one eyebrow – when I've stopped holding my breath. 'I'm Nick, Nicholas Barrat.'

'I know, I've heard all about you,' she says, showing a row of even, pearly-white teeth – *and* she's a natural blue-eyed blonde!

'Ah, my fame has gone before me,' I say, flicking my hair back in that devastating way I have.

'You could say that,' she says, wrinkling her cute nose and glancing at Carrie. Did I detect a wink? Surely not!

She fancies me rotten, no doubt about it.

It seems her options are similar to mine, so I'll see her in English, art and history – yo baby!

Mrs Bailey decides that – seeing as me and Carrie have definitely got the leading parts in *Grease* – we might as well work up a double act using the script and one of the songs. It can be one of our ten minute set pieces, like the one we did last week – the balcony scene from *Romeo and Juliet*. *Grease* is a bit different to Shakespeare but it all goes towards our final assessment.

So . . . I'm stuck in a corner with Carrie, all lesson, while the girl of my dreams is doing a mime with the rest of the group, among them the brutish Beasley, who'd better not lay a sticky finger on her marble-like countenance.

Carrie and me manage to get something going, though, and by break I have something else on my mind.

I get a message. I've to go and see Old Foxy at lunchtime. I suppose he wants to go over my comments after last night's 'imposition', as Mr Liversedge called it. There isn't all that much to discuss. All I did last night was list my own faults – the huge log in my own eye. I think that's what he was getting at, making us look at our own failings. I think the lesson is that we're so busy pointing out other people's faults that we forget to look at our own, or deliberately overlook them. It's a bit like Old Liverish's comment, that day when we were at each other's throats in the Quad: 'If any one of you is without sin, let him be the first to throw a stone . . .'

And that's the lesson, Nicky boy. Admit you have faults and do something about *them* before you start picking spots off brother Chris!

I get it, Foxy, old boy. I get it loud and clear. I spent most of last night's sleepless hours getting it. I didn't realise up till now just what it means to be a Christian. Before it was all talk . . . The Great Nicholas Barrat! . . . But it's Jesus who's GREAT . . . he died for *me*.

I know God has forgiven me for being a prat . . . Trouble is, I'm trying to forgive myself . . . To do things properly, I'll have to change the whole way I go about things, change my image and be the nice guy, especially to Chris. Can you imagine my fan club's reaction to me *apologising* for my unchristian attitude?

But Old Foxy did say that it's *possible* to do the right thing when Jesus transforms our lives . . .

However, I put it out of my mind, for the moment, because it's break and it's 'meeting in the Quad' time.

Carrie's still got the ravishing Rachel in tow, so I saunter over and fix the girl with my 'I'm the guy for you' gaze.

Funny, isn't it? I can make my eyes wet at will, make them all moist and tender-looking, as though I'm weeping silently with suppressed emotion . . . a long-suffering hero who's dying for love.

It's done me proud in one or two sticky moments, this ability to look totally contrite, and it's a real asset when I'm out to impress a girl. They can't resist the soft-hearted sentimental approach – gets them every time. This Rachel chick is just another bird, after all, if just that bit more special. A swan amongst geese?

'Where have you been all my life?' I whisper soft and low, leaning closer with one hand on the wall above her head and the other in my pocket, sort of nonchalant.

'Budleigh Salterton,' she says.

There's no answer to that!

Carrie is doubled up and giggling into a hanky and Rachel's staring at me and waiting for my next comment. There isn't one.

I'm tongue-tied!

Another gaggle of girls arrives to quiz the new girl and I'm out on a limb and ignored as they cluster round her and crowd me out.

This is not on – not on at all!

Anyway, there's always lunch-time – if I don't give Old Foxy too much of my time – *and* the next three lessons, with any luck.

Doom and gloom and no such luck. She's elsewhere! I'm stuck in one general studies group and she's in another. Is there no justice in this world?

I'm in the RE room with Old Liverish. General studies is modular and we move around to cover three areas – health and hygiene, social studies, and religious attitudes to contemporary issues – the last with Old Liverish. It's the only bit of RE we get, if we're not doing it as a GCSE. It's a shame, really, because he's good. I used to enjoy RE in junior school and in the first three years at Cannongate. I thought everybody had to do it, like it says in the National Curriculum, but it seems to take the last place when they do the timetables. I think it's really stupid to cut it down to one lesson a week and none at all after Year Nine. Everybody needs to know what's right and wrong and not everybody goes to church or has parents who bother! Everybody needs to know about God who loves and forgives us when we mess up . . . I've messed up *again* . . . this time with Rachel . . .

In contemporary issues, we discuss things like abortion, euthanasia and racism and Old Liverish doesn't mind us voicing *our* opinions, however wild they are, as long as we are prepared to consider his . . .

I don't find it so easy . . . the loving my neighbour bit. When it all boils down to the nitty-gritty, what Jesus said makes sense in today's world, but it's hard to live up to with sniggering geeks calling you soft and a chicken if you don't act hard.

It's usually a double lesson that flies by, once we get to grips with the subject and he talks a lot of sense, does Old Liverish.

Today, he's on about racial, cultural and religious tolerance and he keeps looking at me!

I'm trying to tolerate my brother – honest!

Mind you, I've almost decided that the easiest way to tolerate Chris is to avoid him, but life's not that easy, is it? I can't avoid him so I'll have to love him.

I'm going to need help! Old Foxy's words come to mind again . . . Jesus will help me . . . no sweat.

At last – although I'm enjoying the debate – the bell goes for lunch and I hotfoot it to the canteen. I've got a full hour before I face Old Foxy and an hour's all I need to have Rachel Gale eating out of my hand.

It's a cinch!

I pop into the lad's cloakroom and run a comb through my squeaky-clean locks, polish my shoes on the back of my school pants and practise my most winning smile. Then I'm off to seek and conquer!

I must look good. The girls are lining the corridors

and swooning against the walls as I pass by, but I have one goal – one treasure to seek – one pearl of great price – Rachel!

She's with Carrie and they're sitting with Chris!

This is *not* bliss!

I have two choices – put aside my vow to stay away from my brother to be near my girl, or stay away from the girl to avoid him!

Quel dommage! Or in common parlance, what a mess-up!

As it happens, it's Carrie that breaks the ice, standing up and waving me over.

I go, because it'll look like sour grapes if I don't, but I ain't a happy chappie, no sirree!

'You've met Rachel . . . in theatre studies,' Carrie says as I sit down.

I nod, too choked to chat.

In my mind's eye I see the paper I did last night – my list of personal logs. There I am, sorting out my failings and almost convincing myself that it's a good thing to talk and tolerate the twit, when what I really want to do is to smack him one in the eye . . . logs and all! He's walking close to the edge – the edge of my fist! Didn't I say I need help?

I'm polite, smile a lot and do my best to get her attention but she only has eyes for him, the nerd!

They're rabbiting on about some geographical spot where somebody's put some windmills. Not real ones that grind corn – those metal stick things with blades that generate power by wind.

Imagine the scene! He's faced with the perfect Helen of Troy, beauty personified, and he's talking wind! How typical!

I'd have talked of love and simple things like taking a

moonlit stroll with Nick the knight . . . Although, the old armour is looking distinctly tarnished after talking to God last night.

Windpower, I ask you!

I give up round about 'steam engines and nuclear fusion' and decide they deserve each other, for the moment. I resolve to have another go at captivating the creature during the afternoon and condescend to allow Chris his moment of joy. It won't last when I really get cracking! I've never lost a lady!

Anyway, I push off at ten to two for my date with destiny, strolling into the outer office as though I haven't a care in the world.

Mavis looks over her specs and shakes her head.

'You, again?' she says, 'What have you done now?'

'Nothing.' I grin. 'We're still sorting out the last evil deed. There's no rest for the wicked, is there?'

'You boys!' she says, and buzzes to tell Old Foxy I've arrived.

He's sitting at his desk and he's got the sheets we handed in to Old Liverish last night. They didn't waste any time getting together! He keeps looking at one paper, then the other, then back to the first one and giving me the odd glance in between.

He's trying to psych me out, the old fox!

I smile – the one that makes me irresistible, I hope!

'You wanted to see me, sir?' I say, flashing my teeth.

He isn't impressed. He looks at me and shakes his head.

'If what you have written here is from the heart, Nick,' he says, 'and if I'm reading between the lines correctly, we don't appear to have a problem. At least, not one that's insurmountable.'

'No, sir,' I mutter.

'According to this list, it's yourself who has all the faults and Chris is totally innocent of any guile, jealousy and animosity.'

'Yes, sir,' I agree, nodding.

'So, what prompted you to list your *own* faults?'

'Logs in the eye, sir,' I tell him.

It's true! Last night, I listed all the things and feelings I'm not proud of. I didn't write anything about Chris. It didn't seem appropriate, somehow.

'So you decided you'd better take a good look at yourself, did you?' Old Foxy goes on, picking at the wound. 'Well – I thought as much!'

He's still looking from one paper to the other and I'm dying to ask him what Chris has put, but I don't. Let sleeping dogs lie!

He grins and shakes his head.

'Some might have expected *you* to suggest knocking the log out of your brother's eye with a well-aimed fist – and that Chris would complain that *your* log is so big it's sticking out of either ear! However – contrary to many of the staff's expectations – it wasn't the case. I was much nearer the mark I think, wasn't I?'

I shrug . . . not the best thing to do in front of our Head, but he seems to have missed the movement and carries on.

'You've both recognised your own failings and neither of you has mentioned the other. I think that's a step in the right direction for the Battling Barrats!'

I'm gobsmacked! He's telling me that Chris has admitted he's a nerd without blaming *me* for anything.

Quelle surprise!

I'm suitably contrite, as well as astonished and wander back to the Quad in a state of mild euphoria. The crisis is over – as far as Old Foxy's concerned. All that remains is to put the matter of a lasting cease-fire to Chris.

It won't be easy!

As soon as I get through the south entrance I see Chris in the Quad – in the *middle* of the Quad – and paired! He's standing with Rachel Gale, tête à tête, and they're obviously an item, parading their twoness for all to see and envy. I give up! It's all over! Not even Nick the Nasty has the gall to nick half of a proclaimed pair! It's just not done!

I steer clear and disappear, unloved and unseen!

It's art, all afternoon and, as I trudge over to Block C with a heavy heart and dragging feet, I'm feeling pretty confused. God *does* care about me . . . I know that now . . .

Then, suddenly, I'm jabbering away . . . 'Jesus help! Help me to *understand*!'

So I've got my faults! I'm still a nice guy, aren't I? I felt better when I was Nick the Nasty taking a rise out of my twerp of a bro . . . oops, sorry!

Let's face it. Once you've looked at yourself, real hard, and spotted the grotty, unlovable bits, it ain't the done thing to pick spots off other people, especially your brother!

Somehow I can't face the still life Mr Swaine has set up. It's a blue jug, two oranges and a sharp knife. Riveting! And anyway, *she* arrives and sets up an easel.

'I'll go up and do some perspective drawing, sir,' I tell The Brain Drain . . . Mr Swaine.

It's my weak point, perspective – and what an admittance *that* is!

He nods his agreement. He never says much, though he does give the occasional grunt.

Above the design studio is a single room with double

98

doors that open out on to the flat roof of C Block, not that we're allowed out there. It started out as a needle-work room but the light's bad because it only has windows on one side, where the door is. But it's excellent for drawing perspective. It's out on a limb and high, so you can see most of the school buildings *and* the gap in the roof over the Quad. You can actually see down into the central area and there's dozens of converging lines, rows of windows and doors, perpendiculars and horizontals that run off into infinity. Plenty of material to get to grips with.

Besides, nobody likes the exercise so I'm on my own.

Not for long, though.

I hear the door open and I glance round to see Carrie Anders creeping in with a drawing board under one arm.

'What are you doing up here all by yourself?' she asks.

'Being by myself!' I say, pointedly.

'Tough!' she says. She sits down next to me, props her board on an easel and looks out through the double glass doors.

'Want to talk about it?' she says.

'About what,' I mutter. 'Perspective drawing on the roof?'

'About your visit to Mr Cunningham at lunch-time. Chris had to go lesson four. He told Rachel.'

'Did he? Bully for him!' I growl, my eyes fixed on the diminishing row of windows along the side of Block B. 'I'll never get this right!'

'Let me look,' Carrie says, and she comes and bends over my board, leaning on my shoulder. 'You haven't sketched in your eye-line, *or* your focal point. If you don't know where you're going, it never will be right.'

She doesn't have to tell me!

She draws a faint line with a dot on it and makes all my horizontal lines converge on the dot. Suddenly the whole picture looks right.

There's a parable here, somewhere lurking in my consciousness. If you get your focus clear – the point of everything – all other things fall into place, don't they? Asking *Jesus* to help me sort out the bad things in me, in my brother and to love my neighbour as much as I love good ol' Nick Barrat. Am I on the right track?

'Thanks,' I mutter, going over her lines with my darker pencil. Part of me seems to have discovered an important truth but another part is feeling even more down in the mouth. Me – Nick Barrat – needing help from a girl? It's a sad day for the macho-man!

'Talk about it, Nick,' Carrie says, pulling her chair closer – and she doesn't mean the perspective.

We sit there, sort of companionable-like, and while we're drawing A and B Blocks and the Quad and everything, I suddenly feel really comfortable. It's as though, with Carrie Anders, I don't have to be anything but me, Nick Barrat. It's mighty strange but I *feel* like talking.

'I've just realised I *am* a dork!' I say, hardly loud enough for her to hear. She doesn't look up from her work but I know she's listening.

'That's not true,' she says.

'It is,' I tell her. 'I've been so busy picking spots off Chris that I've missed what's wrong with me.'

'Like what?' she asks.

'Like I'm jealous. He's got everything going for him – brains, looks and sex-appeal. Look how that Rachel bird fell off her perch as soon as she spotted him! Chris scores the points in everything. He gets As for his work, wins all the sports trophies and pulls the best looking girl in the building.'

I realise what I've said and try to mend it, clumsily.

'She's the best looking *blonde* in the place, I mean. Not actually the best looking over all, counting the brunettes and . . .'

I stop gabbling because Carrie's grinning.

'You're upset because Rachel likes Chris better than you,' she says.

'Everybody likes him better than me!' I moan. 'Mum and Dad do! It's always "Chris this" and "Chris that" to the neighbours.'

'Perhaps you don't give them anything to boast about – don't do anything to make them proud of you. You do project the wrong image, sometimes.'

'Don't you start!' I mutter, rubbing out a roof line so hard that I tear the paper. Best quality paper too! 'They *do* favour him, their golden boy who's going to do great things and make them proud.'

'That's not what Chris thinks.'

'Isn't it?' I ask, getting a bit riled. 'You don't know the half of it! Do you know what he said, once? He said, "They had to have what was delivered when they got you, Nick. They picked me!" That's what Chris thinks!'

I knew it sounded petty and peevish and, almost as I was saying it, I remembered a comment of my own, made not all that long ago: 'Blood's thicker than water, *adopted* brother!' I colour up at the memory of it and Carrie doesn't fail to spot my red neck.

'Six of one and half a dozen of the other?' she suggests, grinning.

I nod, because it's true.

'We'll have to learn to "tolerate our differences and rejoice in our similarities", won't we?' I quote.

'Mr Liversedge?' she asks, and I nod.

'Similarities!' she goes on, turning her paper over. 'Good-looking, handsome even – if in different ways. Witty, talented – again in different areas, and always there to lend a caring hand when needed!' she writes in large print. 'I remember you going out on a limb, Nick, literally! Remember the kittens?'

I remember the kittens!

Some dork had bagged them, tied a rock to the sack and dumped them in the river . . . in full winter flood! Luckily, the stupid moron had left too much rope between the brick and the sack and it was bobbing in the foam, just in the deep bit before the river pours over Psalter's weir. Dicey!

There was only one way to get it – edge out on an overhanging branch and cut the rope. I borrowed a carving knife from a house and edged out over the flood. It wasn't a big branch and I'm no midget, so by the time I was over the bag I was only inches above the water. A crowd collected and there was a cheer when I dumped the bag on the bank and three ginger kittens crawled out, a bit wet and wobbly but still alive. I got an RSPCA commendation for that – though that's not why I did it.

'And Chris?' Carrie was going on. 'Remember all that time he spent with William Platts, that boy in a wheelchair? He taught him how to use a word processor so he could do his work with one finger and even designed a special worktop that fitted on his chair. That was really something!

'You both showed that you care – in different ways, Nick. We all have to use what we've *got*, not wish we had what someone else has.'

She's right, natch!

'Rejoice in our differences?' I say, smiling again.

'Yes, but what are they, really?' she asks. 'Let's

list them.'

She pulls her chair right up to mine, real close, and her hair brushes my cheek. Smells nice!

'Well,' I begin. 'He's dark and I'm fair. He's short and I'm tall. He's brainy and I'm brawny. He's . . .' And by the time I get to, 'He's a nerd and I'm a dork,' we're both laughing and I notice what a very nice girl Carrie Anders is.

Where've I been looking? She's neat, petite and has beautiful big brown eyes – and I've been hunting blondes! What a NERD!

'Listen,' I say, tucking my pencil behind one ear and leaning back, sort of nonchalant. 'There's that bit of a do at the Fellowship on Saturday night. Great music, great eats and very great company. Fancy practising our dance numbers in public?'

'Not if you're going to be the old Nick Barrat!' Carrie says, pretending to sneer. 'You can't treat me like you treat other girls.'

'*Moi*?' I ask, feigning horror. 'I'm Mr Nice-Guy!'

'No, you're not! At least you weren't last time I saw you pick up a girl and then drop her.'

'That Stephanie? It wasn't serious! I was just having a bit of . . .'

'Fun? We're not there to be bits of fun, Nick. Steph's really nice but you didn't bother to find that out. You just wanted something that Chris had, something nice-looking to be seen with. Steph is *great*-looking but she's a person too, and if you'd bothered to ask her you'd have found out that she got ten GCSEs last year, seven of them As.'

'She didn't *sound* as if . . .'

'Face value again, Nick?' she says. 'Steph's just moved here, from Barnsley. She has a regional accent, that's all.'

103

Carrie stops talking. She's staring at me and waiting for me to say something. What can I say? I've no defence except that I'm a prat who can't see further than his nose. She's telling me that girls aren't objects to look at and fight over and I get the picture. Carrie Anders is a lot more than a nice-looking girl.

Suddenly, the prospect of rehearsing and performing *Grease* has become very desirable and, come to think of it, who's Rachel Gale?

'I know my faults,' I tell her. 'But knowing them is part of the battle and with a little help . . . Look, Carrie, up till now I haven't really *thought* about being a Christian. I've gone through the motions when it suited – like a chameleon – but if I'm to follow Jesus' teaching, and really *be* like him, I need to know him better. I need his help and strength, Carrie, I can't do it on my own.'

Carrie's face is glowing – we're talking *radioactive*! – and she's smiling something chronic, as I finish.

I end up like a prat, whingeing, 'Come to the Fellowship with me. Please.'

'On one condition,' she says, wagging a finger at me. (She has very nice hands!)

'Name it!' I reply grinning.

'No more fightin' and feudin' with Chris!'

I *love* him already!

~ 8 ~

Chris

I'm having a bad dream!

I know it's a dream because, on average, headmasters aren't bright green and ten feet tall with tentacles! This green bloke is beating me over the bonce with my brother Nick, who's a log with eyes!

How do I know this log's my brother Nick? Because he's wooden-headed and thick as a plank, ha-ha-ha!

I wake up laughing and wishing I hadn't guzzled a pile of cheese toasties before I went to bed. Always makes me dream, cheese does.

I did something else before I went to bed too. I asked for help.

I didn't get to sleep for ages because I kept thinking about me and Nick. There's another bit – in Mark's Gospel – that I read last night. The disciples are quarrelling about who is the greatest among them. I suppose they meant who is the most important to Jesus and he tells them that whoever wants to be first must put himself last and be everybody's servant. Then he gets a little kid and tells them they have to be pure and humble, like a child. I'm not sure about the humble bit but I imagine it's to do with listening and learning from people who've lived longer and know more.

Before I went to sleep I asked Jesus to help me put others first, especially Nick, and give me the courage to let the change in me *show.*

It's a nice morning and I get dressed feeling pretty good, despite the dreams and a few second thoughts. I don't *really* think Nick's a plank-head – he's OK in small doses – and I'm not sure I can be nice to him with everybody looking on, not *all* the time. They'll think I've gone soft.

I said quite a lot to Old Foxy yesterday. It's funny but, when it came to actually considering and writing down my grievances against Nick, I couldn't think of any – not anything that matters in the great cosmic scheme of things. And as there was nothing serious enough to make an issue of, except stupid things that make me look a right nerd, I listed everything I could see was wrong with *me.* Frightening!

Old Foxy seemed to think it was something to crow about, looking inside myself and admitting my faults – my whacking great logs! I wanted to ask him what Nick had written but it didn't seem the time or the place.

As it happened, after a boring lecture about living and working together, supporting each other in our trials and tribulations and generally getting on with the business of being brothers etc, etc – as if I don't know all that already – he lets on that Nick listed all *his* faults and never mentioned me!

So there's a thing to think about. All this time I've been grumbling and grousing about a brother who's not half as bad as I've painted him. I really expected him to save himself at my expense. You just never know, do you?

Anyway — I get up, sweating a bit because of the dream and the prospects of a humbling day, and head for the bathroom. There's nobody else up, not even Mum, because it's early. Although it's Saturday, Mum still gets up at seven, being a day person, like me. Once I'm awake I have to get up or I start twitching to be doing something constructive.

I'm having a nice, leisurely wash and brush-up and I'm just dealing with the sparkling choppers when there's a knock on the bathroom door.

Guess who?

I wait for the threats and the promises of dire deeds to come if I don't 'shift it and quick!' but they don't happen. Am I still dreaming?

'Chris?' Nick whispers.

I'm stunned! He's trying not to wake the parents. How uncommonly thoughtful of the chap!

'What?' I whisper back.

'Will you be long?' he whispers, a bit louder.

'Give me five,' I say, frothily.

'Right,' he says, and all is quiet on the bathroom front!

Isn't this a turn up for the book? *I'm* on the inside, *he's* on the outside and he's not threatening to terminate me if I don't vacate the premises *tout de suite*!

Our visits to Old Foxy seem to have altered quite a few things in our otherwise humdrum and predictable lives. Nick's being nice and I'm hurrying to accommodate him. Everything's all pleasant and right with the world . . . our little bit of it at least.

I suppose we've both been led to take a good long look at ourselves. I've called Nick some awful things, in the past and — when it boils down to it — most of them undeserved. It's no wonder he doesn't fancy me as a brother.

I've been looking at him and expecting him to be like me and he isn't. He's big, brawny and boastful Nick Barrat and he's a nice guy, everybody says so. Who am I to think different?

I think, if I'm honest, that there's a good bit of the old 'green-eye' syndrome lurking in my murky depths. I'm jealous of the way he seems to saunter through life without a care in the world.

I've got so much to worry about like, what if I don't get enough GCSEs and A levels to get me where I want to be? Nick doesn't want to be *anywhere* so he's not stressed about work and exams. Sometimes I wish I could be like him! I'm jealous of the way he gets the girls as well. They migrate his way without him *trying* to net them.

I've always had this feeling that, being 'different' I have to prove myself – prove I'm as good as the next. What a load of old rubbish! When I tried to write down the times Nick has been shown preference over me, at school as well as at home, I couldn't think of any – not anything important. You can't write down that he once got new shoes and I didn't or that he got the biggest apple three weeks last Thursday, without being a bigger prat than he is – was!

It was all in my mind.

This 'logs in the eye' business should be brought to everybody's notice. Think what a difference it would make in the House of Commons! When they televise a sitting it appears to be little more than a slanging match between the honourable members with the Speaker yelling, 'Order! Order!' every ten seconds. She has a voice like a fog-horn and needs it! It's worse than our

Quad at break! Instead of the Tories listing Labour's faults and vice versa, they could put up or shut up – get down to sorting out the country's problems together. They should be overlooking personal quirks and working together towards peace and harmony. I think I'll write and suggest they do a bit of pertinent reading!

At breakfast it's 'snap-crackle-pop' and sunshiny faces all round. Dad is beaming all over his face because he's just landed a contract with the council – maintaining the 'Toby-adge-fis' (that's how you pronounce it). That's what Grandad used to call all tractors, dustbin lorries, earth movers and other lumbering vehicles like drain-dredgers and road sweepers with noisy engines and pipes hanging all over the place. Hence, a T.O.B.I.A.J.F.E. . . . 'A Thing Of Beauty Is A Joy For Ever'. Daft what some families have as 'specialnesses', isn't it? As Mum always says, 'beauty is in the eye of the beholder', and Grandad beheld machines!

Mum, who's rarely down in the dumps, is rushing around collecting old rubber gloves, trowels and garden forks and stowing them in a wooden trug, along with her sun hat and specs. What gives?

'Remember your promise!' she says, popping out of her 'gathering' mode to dole out scrambled eggs.

'Promise?' Nick says, glancing at me and raising those devastating eyebrows.

'Don't go all wide-eyed and innocent on me!' Mum says. 'You promised Mr Sanderson you'd help tidy the church grounds, remember? Today's the day!'

I groan, inwardly.

Outwardly, I add *my* smile to everybody else's.

'It's a lovely day for it,' I say brightly. I *had* forgotten! At least I haven't made other plans.

Half an hour later, we're all trudging in the general

direction of St Kentigern's. Dad drops off at his garage and Mum makes a detour to the shops, so me and Nick arrive on our own, complete with basket.

'There you are!' The Rev says, grinning and rubbing his hands together.

Mrs Sanderson comes up behind him and she's all flushed from carrying The Rev Junior on one hip. It's a boy but it's hard to tell when it's wearing a sun-bonnet and dungarees.

Nick points out the Aussie twins he looked after and suggests, in sign language, that we avoid them like the plague. At least, I *think* that's what a cut throat and rolling eyes means. A variety of wrinklies in various stages of health are bobbing about among the bushes. They do need us young 'uns!

Everybody gets a patch to pretty up and me and Nick are assigned a weed-ridden wedge where the transept juts out from the nave.

Nick looks at me and I look at Nick.

'Pax?' he says.

'Can you hack it?' I ask.

'I managed this morning,' he replies, grinning. 'You performed *votre toilette sans* interference!'

'True,' I nod. 'And your *français* has improved.'

'Life's too short,' he says.

'And too interesting,' I add.

He winks and without further ado we get stuck in, bent-backed, to battle with the brambles.

Time passes at express rate and when The Rev appears with glasses of orange juice we've made quite an impact on the habitat.

'You work well together,' The Rev says, eyeing our handiwork. 'It's amazing what can be done with a bit of teamwork and the right tools.'

110

He's beaming and nodding and rubbing his hands together like Fagin on a good day. He's well pleased!

'Willing horses make light work!' Mr Simpson observes as he passes us with a barrow full of potted plants. 'When you've dug it over you can take some of these. They'll fare well in that sheltered corner.'

Dug it over? What do they want, blood?

We do work well as a team, though; me raking the tangle and snipping the stems while Nick, all trowel and brute force, uproots the 'toughies' and hauls them away.

'Like a pair of horses in harness,' The Rev says. 'Each pulling his share of the weight with a will.'

'Who's this "Will" bloke?' Nick asks, with a broad grin, and I sling a clod at him, but only in fun.

The Rev 'tut-tuts' and wanders off so we both take a rest — to down the juice — and lean against the brick wall. It's warm on my back. Nick grins at me, all orangey round his lips, and I grin back as we perform the 'Yo Bro' hand-slapping routine.

'Do you think we're getting on because you've stopped being a dork?' I ask . . . not with any menace, you understand.

'Nah!' says Nick. 'You've stopped wearing blinkers, that's all.'

'About these specks and logs,' I say, squatting comfortably on the stone foundation ledge at the base of the wall.

Nick joins me. 'What about them?' he says.

'I know I've got irritating habits and I'm not what you might call tolerant,' I begin, trying to clean the slate.

'Don't worry about it,' Nick says, pulling a length of grass to chew. 'I'm not easy to tolerate, being a big-headed bozo.'

'I'm sorry about Rachel. I know you fancied her but,

we just got on so well and . . .'

'Don't worry about that either,' he says. 'I've decided that, as it's gentlemen that prefer blondes and I'm just an ordinary dork, I'd better go for brunettes.'

'Any old brunette or somebody special?' I ask, tossing him a stick of chewy.

'I've just noticed Carrie Anders,' Nick says, and his eyes go all soft and sentimental.

'Great, she's nice,' I tell him, adding, 'I'm taking Rachel to the rave tonight,' because it seems like a good time to drop it into the conversation – the first *real* talk we've had for months.

'Brilliant!' he says. 'We'll make up a foursome,' and then we get back to the planting of purple petunias.

By half past six, I'm shampooed and shiny-shod with just a splash of aftershave applied to the chops. Nick thinks I don't need to shave but he can think again. The old top lip gets hairy every other day – unlike *his* baby face – and a splash of aftershave doesn't go amiss.

Mind you, when Nick really goes all out, there's no wonder he has the girls swooning. I hate to say it but he's one great-looking guy.

But – I'm the one with the best looking girl in town!

It's an excellent night. Spot on! The four of us get on like a house on fire and it's a load of laughs. I've always liked Carrie, as a friend. She's the sort of girl you can have an intelligent conversation with and she seems to have toned Nick down a bit. He's funny, good company, he hasn't told us how brilliant he is – not once – *and* hasn't so much as glanced at another girl all night. That's new, for him and I have a quiet word with Carrie when Nick goes for bottles of Coke and Rachel's in the ladies.

'What have you done to him?' I ask her.

She grins and shakes her head.

'It's not just him,' she says. 'You're both different . . . and nicer!'

Round about half nine, Nick and Carrie go for a snack and I take the floor with the girl of my dreams. We're moving to the beat and standing as close as we dare, with The Rev looking on, when this big guy comes up, elbows me out of the way and starts drooling all over Rachel.

I don't recognise the geek but he's well hard and I noticed The Rev's looking a bit perturbed.

'Do you mind?' I say, ever so politely. 'We were dancing together.'

'Not any more you're not,' the bozo says with real menace. 'Butt off!'

Now that isn't nice! There's several things I can do at this point, so I choose the most dangerous.

'I said she's with me,' I tell him again, and I make the mistake of pulling at his jacket.

Rachel's gone pale and, although the geek's a foot taller and can give me a couple of kilos, I stand my ground.

Another mistake!

Without saying anything, the guy punches me, smack on the nose and there's blood all over the shop. It doesn't take much to give me a nose bleed, I'm prone to them. That's why I usually leg it, fast, when trouble's a-brewing. I hate the sight of blood – when it's mine!

I'm no craven coward, though. I wait till I see The Rev lead Rachel away before I make a dash for the loos. I can't do anything until I've stopped the bleeding and that takes cold, wet toilet paper – oodles of it. The last thing I see is the gatecrasher being hustled outside by the DJ and our organist, Mr Piper . . . don't laugh! It's really his name.

As I've said, I'm no coward. As soon as I've stopped the nosebleed and checked the old hooter's not bent, I go looking for the geek; just to make sure he's off the premises and beyond the point of no return.

Trouble is, when I get outside he isn't on his own. There's four of 'em, now, and all as big and ugly as him.

Now, I'm not averse to wading in for my lady's honour, when it's a fair fight, but four to one is a bit over the odds don't you think?

I'm just wondering how to extricate myself from this unpleasant scenario, when I remember asking Jesus for help last night . . . to put others first . . . But *this* load of yobbos aren't even worth thinking about . . . or are they?

The next moment, as I'm praying that same prayer again, I feel a presence – a warm and comforting shoulder – and I don't have to look to know it's my brother, Nick.

All sorts of things buzz through my brain in the next nanosecond. Don't they say that all your life passes in front of your eyes before you shake off the mortal coil?

I don't get my *whole* life as a movie but I hear myself saying some terrible things I shouldn't have even thought, let alone voiced. Things like, 'You're rubbish, Nick, a loser . . . you're just a pig-headed dork . . . "I'm not my brother's keeper!" '

I may be wrong, but at this moment he seems to be acting as mine!

Four against two is marginally better.

Nothing happens for an age and a half. Then, the leader of the gang takes a step forward. I suppose it's a signal for battle to commence and I prepare to get thumped to bits, hoping that Nick takes the first swing and floors the brute.

He doesn't.

You know those movies where, at moments of crisis, time seems to stop, almost, and all the action is in slow motion? Well, that's what *really* happens!

I can't hear a thing except a steady thud-thud and I realise it's my old ticker, pumping up a storm.

Nick takes a very slow step forward but he has both hands in his pockets. What's he got, a death wish? They'll murder him!

I step forward, level with him. Whither he goes, *I* go, but I close my eyes as the pack leader raises his fist. Here comes the crunch. Not the nose, please, not the nose!

Nothing happens. Then, suddenly after the hush, Nick's talking, slow and gentle-like.

'I'm not going to fight,' he says and my insides hit my boots. 'It's neither the place nor the time. But if you insist, aim for the chin. I've got a great nose and I'd like to keep it.'

I can't believe it, snapping open my eyes to see Nick grinning, still with his hands on his pockets, and bozo-bonce absolutely gobsmacked.

'You having me on?' he grunts.

'Certainly not,' Nick says. 'But me and my brother are out partying, not looking for a punch-up.'

'It's what you're going to get!' the yobbo says.

'Could be,' Nick goes on, nodding slowly. 'But you'll be the only one taking part. We're all members of a Christian Fellowship, here, and one thing we don't do is fight. It isn't our way.'

At that point Rachel comes and stands next to me; even links her arm through mine.

'I would have danced with you if you'd asked properly,' she says. 'But no girl likes to be treated like a piece of furniture. You'd get more response if you were polite and friendly.'

The geek doesn't know what to do. He's up front, the leader, and he doesn't know what's hit him! Certainly not Nick, who's grinning amiably. And boy! Am I proud! ... of Rachel, of Nick and of Carrie, who's joined us. Now we're four to four.

Best of all — I'm *proud* to be a Christian — to be a follower of Jesus. I mouth a silent, 'Thanks!'

'There's a great crowd inside and plenty of girls to go round, as long as you dance and don't split couples up,' Nick tells him.

He, the geek, thinks a bit before he answers. You can almost hear the computer doing a word search! 'OK,' he grunts, eventually. 'The name's Jake!' (It would be, wouldn't it?) 'Who's running the rave?'

All this time, I haven't said a word. Nick's been doing all right on his own. He's turned the other cheek all right and it works! Jesus sure had the right idea!

'We're all members of St Kentigern's Church,' I say to the other three gatecrashers, waiting for the grins and snorts but there aren't any.

'And you're not supposed to fight?' one of them says.

Nick and I look at each other and should be blushing with embarrassment. We haven't exactly lived up to the Christian example in the past, have we?

'Nobody's perfect,' I say. 'But we do try, especially here at the Fellowship. We're having our Whitsuntide bash . . . but not literally!'

'Can we come in then? There's nothing to do anywhere else and the music sounds good,' Jake says. 'We can pay.'

'Be our guests,' Nick invites, winking at me as he waves them in.

We have a great night. Jake, whose real name's John

Sellers, know all there is to know about motorbike maintenance and has a complete set of The Eagles CDs – my favourite group of all time.

Nick surprises me. He makes them welcome, is charming to Rachel and we're having fun, like we did when we were kids.

The Rev buys them all a drink and we discover he used to own a Harley. They enthusiastically discuss the merits of various machines. You can tell he's challenged by the prospect of guiding some lost sheep to the fold.

What he doesn't realise is that he already has two who've been straying a bit! . . . Or perhaps he does, along with a lot of other people like the Head and Old Liverish. Perhaps *I* was the only one with blinkers?

Anyway, we make a great night of it and there's a whole summer ahead to enjoy, as soon as I've got my GCSEs out of the way.

Later, as we're going up to bed after telling Mum and Dad what a brilliant night it's been, I ask Nick something that's been puzzling me.

'Why did you step in and back me up? You never have done before!'

'You've always done a runner, before,' Nick says. 'I'd have waded in if you were really in trouble.'

'To save me from a bashing?'

'Nah! To save you for myself. Nobody bashes my brother, but me!' he says, and he goes into his room, grinning.

I stand on the landing. Nick's CD goes on and it doesn't sound too bad. '*Welcome to the Hotel California*,' somebody sings. It's The Eagles! He's filched one of my CDs the . . .

I'm one step from his door when I pull up sharp. So what? He can't hurt it and, for once, he's listening to some classic stuff! After all – he's my brother, isn't he?

There's one more thing I need to do before I turn in. I need to go downstairs.

There's something I have to get off my chest, whatever Dad does when I've said it. The new Chris Barrat wants to start off with a clean slate, so here goes.

'Dad, have you got a minute?'

~ *9* ~

Rashers, raspberries and remembering

Things were always a little different on Sundays.

For one thing, Mr Barrat had a day of rest. He could have added quite a bit to the family coffers if he'd opened up, as his mechanics were always trying to persuade him to do. He would have had to pay them time-and-a-half but that would be compensated for by running a breakdown service – for all those Sunday drivers who insisted on filling the motorways and breaking down at the drop of a hat – something they'd suggested several times. There was a lot of money to made on Sunday, they said, but Mr Barrat wouldn't hear of it.

'I make a decent living six days out of the seven and I pay you well over the going rate. If I have to miss a day with my family and a visit to my church to be a millionaire, I can do without it, thank you very much!'

The day was special for Mrs Barrat too. Apart from her weekly visit to the Fairlawn Nursing Home – to spend some time with Mrs Tyler, who used to live next door – she had a lie in and went to the evening service

119

with the family. She called for Grandad Barrat on the way.

Chris and Nick went in the morning, to the Youth Fellowship gathering.

Every other morning, Mrs Barrat was up at seven with breakfast on the go, the washer rumbling away and Mr Barrat's lunch-box and flask at the ready. There was a drinks machine at the works but it didn't make coffee the way he liked it, strong and sweet. In fact, nobody could make or cook *anything* as well as his wife!

On Sundays, though, it was Mr Barrat who manned the roomy dining-kitchen. It was still early, eight thirty or so, but he gave his wife an extra hour or two in bed while he fried rasher after rasher of bacon and everything that was lying around in the fridge . . . and one or two things that shouldn't have been!

Once, and he'd never lived it down, he'd tossed a plastic tomato slice into the pan with gruesome results – though how it came to *be* in the fridge in the first place remained an unsolved mystery.

Usually, by a quarter to nine he had everything within ten minutes of perfection – in his own estimation – and that's when he called the boys.

Sometimes, both Chris and Nick wished they could be left alone to surface when they felt like it. Gaz Cooper strolled downstairs at lunch-time and, once, after a Saturday visit to an air show and a sleep-over at his friend's house, Chris had been horrified to find himself in bed and half the day gone. Chris didn't want to waste the day sleeping *or* miss Fellowship, he just wanted to do his own thing, upstairs, without the breakfast ritual.

Nick always grumbled that he wouldn't mind spending all day in his bed, as long as he had music and a Coke or two, like Tim Gudgeon said *he* did on Sundays.

But the one time he'd had the opportunity – a heavy cold and a headache – he'd insisted on going to church as usual. He might miss something important.

In spite of both their protestations however, once downstairs and plied with bacon, sausage, fried egg, mushrooms, beans, tomatoes and hash-browns – not to mention fried bread – the effort of getting up seemed worth it.

Mrs Barrat had breakfast in bed on Sundays. Not the plate of killer-calories and fatty fry-ups that faced the boys, but healthy cereal, unsweetened fruit juice and a boiled egg – just as she liked it. Mrs Barrat was just a little conscious of an extra inch or two, here and there, that she'd prefer to do without.

Nick and Chris grinned at each other as their dad put the finishing touches to Mum's tray – a single flower in a slender vase. He'd been doing that for as long as they could remember, and probably long before that. He even took care with what he planted in the garden, so there'd always be *something* that was colourful or sweet-smelling.

This Sunday morning, it was a slender sprig of honeysuckle from the climbing plant that had just begun to bloom by the back window.

'There!' Mr Barrat said, picking up the tray. 'That looks nice, doesn't it? Mum'll like that!'

He'd said *that* every Sunday, too.

'I told Dad, last night,' Chris said, when he was sure Mr Barrat was out of earshot.

'Told him what?' Nick mumbled, his mouth full of fried potato.

'About me making that hoax call, to the police.'

Nick's eyebrows shot up. 'I'd forgotten about that in all the excitement! What did he say?' he asked.

'Not a lot,' Chris replied, toying with a rather overdone sausage that was resisting his knife. 'He said he'd *thought* it might be one of us.'

'He didn't!'

'He did. And when I asked him why he hadn't said anything – hauled us in if he suspected one of us – he said he knew we'd tell him ourselves, eventually; if it *was* one of us – or both.'

'Didn't he go mad . . . bust a gasket?'

Chris shook his head and bent to pick up the sausage that had skittered off his plate and on to the floor.

'We ought to get a dog, if Dad doesn't improve,' he said, staring at the escapee that sat on the end of his fork.

'It's the new frying pan, he can't seem to get the hang . . . forget the flippin' sausage, Chris! What did he say?'

Chris sighed and pushed his plate away, suddenly losing his appetite.

'He said we all make mistakes and act a bit thoughtless at times – and we'll all have a long talk, later. I feel a right nit!'

'I've been pointing that out to you for years,' Nick said. 'But you didn't believe me. Do you think he'll ground you?'

'Sure to – and it'll serve me right. Just when I've got a really nice girl,' Chris said dejectedly. 'I'm pig sick!'

'I'll say I put you up to it. I did, in a way,' Nick said. 'A trouble shared and all that.'

'Thanks, Nick, but it's up to me. I'm the dork that did it!'

'Hey! *I'm* the dork! You're the *nerd*, remember?'

'Actually, we're a pair of *dweebs*,' Chris said, grinning.

They were clearing away when Mr Barrat came back downstairs. He was carrying a shirt and he was frowning, not smiling.

'Mum discovered this, in the laundry basket,' he said, holding the thing aloft with finger and thumb. 'There's blood on it!'

'Ah!' Chris said.

'Ah?' Mr Barrat echoed. 'Is that all you have to say . . . ah?'

'No, Dad. It's mine,' Chris said. 'I meant to put it to soak but . . .'

'But you forgot?'

'It was just a nosebleed, that's all,' Chris said. 'The first one for ages. I'll put it to soak.'

'A nosebleed, eh? Nosebleeds usually drip downwards – it's called gravity! This is what I would call a splatter! Your mum thought you might have been fighting,' Mr Barrat said, watching Chris get a plastic bucket and fill it with cold water. 'You should have done that last night, when gravity failed after the fight you didn't have!'

'Who would we fight?' Nick cried, raising both hands inquiringly.

'Each other?' Mr Barrat suggested, filling the sink with hot water.

'Dad – we're brothers!' Chris protested and at that moment Mr Barrat squeezed the last drop from the plastic bottle of washing-up liquid and it came out with a 'raspberry' sound that seemed to qualify Chris's statement.

Both boys tried to suppress their mirth but, to their surprise, Dad was chuckling too and he squeezed the bottle again, just for good measure.

'Show me two brothers, or sisters for that matter, who don't have their ups and downs,' he said, rubbing at the first plate with a little mop on a stick. 'It's been the norm since Cain did for Abel!'

'Actually, Dad,' Chris said, deciding to come clean. 'I did get punched, once, but not by Nick. There was a bit of trouble at the Fellowship do last night, but it didn't come to anything . . . not a fight, anyway. Nick saw to that.'

'Just a bit of a rumble, was it?'

'Just a bit,' Chris said. 'There was this older kid, Jake, who tried to butt in on me and Rachel and it got a bit out of hand but we sorted it and had a great night, including Jake and his gang.'

'But you have had your moments, you and Nick,' Mr Barrat said, handing Chris a plate.

'Some,' he nodded.

'It's only natural,' Mr Barrat said. 'It's nothing to be ashamed of, as long as you sort it, eventually. We wouldn't be human if we didn't have opinions, and some opinions are worth fighting for . . . but most of us draw the line at fratricide.'

'Cain and Abel?' Nick asked, grinning.

'No, me and *my* only brother, your Uncle Harry. I felt like strangling him at times!' Mr Barrat grinned, good-humouredly, and the boys relaxed.

Everybody sat down and Mr Barrat poured himself the last dregs from the teapot, settling himself for one of his trips down memory lane.

Chris and Nick recognised the signs and waited.

'When your Uncle Harry and me were boys,' he began, his eyes turned up to contemplate the ceiling. 'We had the same sort of thing going – but we had notches, not stripes. We cut a notch on the back gate every time one of us took a rise out of the other. *And* we had strict rules! No harm to insects, reptiles, birds or animals; no upsetting Ma and no annoying Pa if he was within striking distance! Anything else was fair game.

124

Three notches in a row meant a forfeit by the lagger, the one behind. It meant parting with a treasured marble or something equally precious or the handing over of the weekly bag of toffees – for a month! How we strove to keep our toffees – to keep level!

'One time – we were about ten and eight, I think, Harry being the elder – we were dropping sticks over the canal bridge and waiting for them to come out the other side. They never moved much, except when something had been through the locks or a barge passed, but we liked the game. Well, a narrow boat came along, with two barges behind. There aren't any now, but in those days they were a regular sight on our stretch of canal.'

'Pulled by a horse?' Chris asked.

'I'm not *that* old!' Mr Barrat said. 'Give us a break! They had engines – but only went about four miles an hour, if that.

' "Let's jump on it," our Harry said, and before I'd time to tell him no, he'd climbed over and was tottering on a three-inch ledge, just over the tunnel opening. The actual narrow boat was in front and towed behind it were two open barges, one behind the other, full of coal.

' "Don't Harry," I said, but I hardly got it out before he'd gone – dropped off the ledge and was slithering and sliding on the coal.

' "Come on, jump!" he yells and there's nothing else to do but go for it, or look a twerp! By the time I'd got the nerve to jump, the barge was nearly through and I landed half on coal and half on the back-board. What a whack I took, right on the ankle bone!'

'How far did you go?' Nick asked. 'Were you spotted?'

'No. We got down on the back-board, hidden by the coal and, for a while, it was fun – trailing our hands in the mucky water and watching the odd duck paddling about. There were a few folks on the bank but they must have thought we were the bargee's kids, we were mucky enough, so they didn't take much notice.

'Trouble was – and we were too young and daft to work it out – the coal was going to Redfearns, the glassworks, and it's miles! We got hungry and thirsty and my ankle swelled up like a balloon. I daren't take my boot off in case I never got it on again!

'Then, it got worse.

'Suddenly, we're out of the canal and into the basin. It's choppy and the barges are rolling this way and that . . .' Mr Barrat paused, shaking his head at the memory.

'And?' Nick prompted.

'And, before I knew it, I'm in the drink and going under. Harry's frozen with fright, the bargee's up front – two boats away – and I'm in heavy boots and a thick jacket. I thought I was a goner! The water was so black and mucky I couldn't see a thing. I remember thinking I should've let him go, let him get "three up" and pay the forfeit. As it was, I could see me without toffees ever again!

'Anyway, I bobbed up for the third and last time, feeling all woosy, and I'm hauled on to the wharf, half-dead and dripping. I was lucky. Two glass blowers were just taking a break and having a smoke outside and they got me out with a boat hook. What a jaunt *that* was!'

'Did you get grounded?' Chris asked.

'Grounded? You didn't get grounded in those days, boy! You got a good skelping and you couldn't sit down for a week. You don't know you're born, these days.'

'Grandad walloped you?' Nick said.

'Not on your life, boy! We limped home, walking a

bit and thumbing the odd lift on a lorry or two – and *that's* something you can't do in safety, these days! We were a bit late for tea but we made some excuse, I can't remember just what.'

'You've never told us that one before,' Nick said.

'I haven't told you lots of things – might have given you ideas, not that you haven't had enough of your own!'

'You *weren't* perfect then, Dad?' Chris said, grinning.

'Nobody's perfect, Chris. Actually, Harry got into more trouble than me, that time, him being covered in coal dust. I'd been doused and had drip-dried by the time we got home.'

'Is that a true story, Dad?' Nick asked, wondering if it hadn't been made up to make a point.

'Every word!' Mr Barrat said. 'We got up to things you wouldn't believe. If my ma and pa had known the half of it, they'd have had a fit! You can ask Uncle Harry, if you like. He'll tell you. Now, let's forget our mad moments, for now, and get these pots finished.'

He washed, Chris wiped and Nick stowed everything away.

'We used to take risks on the canal,' Nick said, as he hung the frying pan on its hook.

'You didn't – I did!' Chris exclaimed, throwing the tea towel at Nick's head. 'You always wanted me to go first!'

'Of course,' Nick replied, grinning. 'Who keeps a dog and barks himself? I had to see if it was safe!'

'So that's why it was always Chris who came home wet through,' Mr Barrat said. 'Just like me and Harry!'

'When did you stop?' Nick asked.

'Stop what – falling in the canal?' Mr Barrat said, pulling the plug out and letting the water drain away.

'No! When did you stop trying to go one better than

each other. Trying to be top dog?' Nick said.

'When we realised we were stuck with each other, how much we needed and loved each other, how much we were upsetting Ma and Pa and . . .' Mr Barrat paused and looked from Nick to Chris and back again. 'And when I stopped seeing *his* faults, took a good long look at my own and prayed for the Lord's forgiveness and help!' he added

'Logs in the eye?' Chris asked, looking at Nick.

'Logs!' Nick agreed. 'And a whole lot of help from our friends.'

'Yes. It's more than just recognising your own faults!' Mr Barrat said. 'It's forgiving each other and being there for each other, with the Lord's help. Although we'd never *seemed* close, Harry was right there when I *really* needed support. All our rivalry and antagonism ended with one particular incident – and *that* was over a certain girl!'

Mr Barrat was facing the door, as he spoke, and suddenly his eyes widened and his neck, ears and cheeks turned bright red. Mrs Barrat was standing in the doorway holding her breakfast tray.

'What certain girl?' she asked.

There was a moment of silence.

'Rachel . . . Carrie,' Chris and Nick said simultaneously, to cover up for their dad and his youthful memories, while he, about to protest that it was all a very long time ago, smiled and said nothing.